# THE REVENGE FILES

### including
## BUGS ON THE BRAIN
### and
## DEAD DAD DOG

# Jamie Rix

Illustrated by Nigel Raines

**Corgi Yearling Books**

Further revenges by Alistair Fury (and Jamie Rix!):

*The Kiss of Death*
*Tough Turkey*
*Summer Helliday*
*Exam Fever*

And for younger readers by Jamie Rix,
published by Young Corgi:

*One Hot Penguin*
*Mr Mumble's Fabulous Flybrows*

Also by Jamie Rix:

*Grizzly Tales For Gruesome Kids*
*Ghostly Tales For Ghastly Kids*
*Fearsome Tales For Fiendish Kids*
*More Grizzly Tales For Gruesome Kids*
*fatherchristmas.con*
*Johnny Casanova - the unstoppable sex machine*
*The Changing Face of Johnny Casanova*
*The Cool Guide*
*The Fire In Henry Hooter*
*Free The Whales*
*The Last Chocolate Biscuit*
*Looking After Murphy*
*Giddy Goat*

BUGS
ON THE
BRAIN

THE REVENGE FILES
A CORGI YEARLING BOOK 0 440 86681 2

Originally published in Corgi Yearling as *The War Diaries of Alistair Fury:
Bugs on the Brain* and *The War Diaries of Alistair Fury: Dead Dad Dog*

Corgi Yearling edition published 2005

1 3 5 7 9 10 8 6 4 2

Copyright © Jamie Rix, 2005
Illustrations copyright © Nigel Baines, 2005

*The War Diaries of Alistair Fury: Bugs on the Brain*
Copyright © Jamie Rix, 2002
Illustrations copyright © Nigel Baines, 2002

*The War Diaries of Alistair Fury: Dead Dad Dog*
Copyright © Jamie Rix, 2002
Illustrations copyright © Nigel Baines, 2002

Corgi Yearling Books are published by Random House Children's Books,
61–63 Uxbridge Road, London W5 5SA,
a division of The Random House Group Ltd,
in Australia by Random House Australia (Pty) Ltd,
20 Alfred Street, Milsons Point, Sydney, NSW 2061, Australia,
in New Zealand by Random House New Zealand Ltd,
18 Poland Road, Glenfield, Auckland 10, New Zealand,
and in South Africa by Random House (Pty) Ltd,
Endulini, 5A Jubilee Road, Parktown 2193, South Africa

THE RANDOM HOUSE GROUP Limited Reg. No. 954009
www.kidsatrandomhouse.co.uk

A CIP catalogue record for this book is available from the British Library.

Printed and bound in Great Britain by Cox & Wyman Ltd

To Jonty
(or should I say Alistair?)

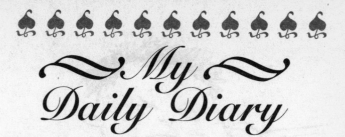

# My Daily Diary

This diary belongs to <u>Alistair Fury</u>
Age <u>11</u>
Address <u>47 Atrocity Road, Tooting,</u>
<u>England</u>
Favourite Colour <u>Not pink!</u>
Favourite Boy Band <u>Oh no, is this a</u>
<u>drippy girl's diary?</u>
Cuddly Teddy Bear's Name <u>It is! That's</u>
<u>just typical! Everything in my life is</u>
<u>double pants with extra pongy cheese!</u>
Person You Would Most
Like to Kiss <u>Oh perlease!</u>
<u>Person You Would Most Like to kill -</u>

## William and Mel

## Notes

I am a sweet little brother, innocent of all wrong and doer only of good deeds. Butter doesn't melt in my mouth. I am keeping this secret diary so that other little brothers in the world will know that they are not alone in being the most unloved and persecuted human life form on the planet. Is there *anybody* out there who loves us?

Sometimes, when poor little me is tortured by the vicious half-nelsons, dead legs and ear twists of my big brother (who's a lazy cheating liar), and the poisonous tongue and towel slaps of my big sister (who says she loves every boy in the world *except* me), I am forced to get even in any way I can. It is my hope that some of my revenge tactics might prove useful to other little brothers faced with evil brothers and sisters who are twice their size and half their intelligence!

# NERVOUS READERS BEWARE

Some readers may be shocked by the appalling physical and mental torture to which I am subjected by my big brother and sister on a daily basis. Some may think me heroic and wonderful for suffering this torture without a word of complaint. Some may want to send me money or put a statue of me up in Trafalgar Square. Some may even want to liken me to Gandhi or Jesus. But if it's a toss up, just send the money, because I'm saving up for a motorbike when I'm sixteen.

And handsome too, if you could see me

ALISTAIR THE GREAT

# SATURDAY

We were in the tent in my garden.

'It's so unfair! My name is Alistair not Alice!' I cried. There were nearly tears in my eyes. My best friends, Aaron and Ralph, could see that I was suffering. We were sleeping in the Great Outdoors like wild bear trappers, only with the back door of the house open in case we needed the loo or got scared. I'd already been into the house four times. Once for blankets, once for fly spray, once for a 'spider hammer' and once for crisps. I was telling my best friends how utterly awful and tragic my life was as a little brother and they were listening and nodding in agreement.

By the way, Ralph had eaten so many chocolate biscuits that he'd been sick in a little puddle just outside the tent door.

We'd been out to have a look at it twice already, because Aaron wanted to see how quickly the flies would eat it.

'My big brother was allowed to stay out in a tent when he was *five*,' I said indignantly. 'I'm eleven and this is my first time! I mean, that's not fair, is it?'

'What about your big sister?' said Ralph.

'What *about* my big sister?' I said. 'When I was three, she was good at making pasta pictures, but otherwise I hate her. She's so boring about her beautiful new boyfriend.'

# THE BEAUTIFUL NEW BOYFRIEND

His name is Luke, but Mel calls him Luke the Nuke, because she thinks he's dynamite! **Ugh!** Luke the Puke more like, because they spend all their time snogging!

Also, Mel says she wants to be an actress, but I know that's just so she can get on Mum's telly show when she knows it's *my* turn!

'You're going on telly?' gasped Aaron, when I told him that.

'William did it last year, but he's not cute anymore like me. He's got bigger and hairier and treats me like a slave! Mum said if I was well behaved for the whole next month she'd ask her producer.'

You should have seen the look of envy on my best friends' faces.

'But you'll be famous!' said Ralph.

'Yup! With my first million I'm buying a supermodel and a Ferrari Testosterone!'

'I know why they call you Alice,' said Aaron suddenly. He's never been quick off the mark. 'Maybe there was a mix-up at the hospital when you were born. Maybe the baby your mother gave birth to was a boy,

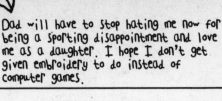

Dad will have to stop hating me now for being a sporting disappointment and love me as a daughter. I hope I don't get given embroidery to do instead of computer games.

but the baby they took home was a girl and they've never noticed!'

'You mean underneath all my dangly bits I'm really a girl?' I said.

'Question,' said Ralph. 'Did you cry at *The Ugly Duckling* first time you read it?'

'Yes,' I said, 'I did.'

'Girl,' he said.

I was stunned. I didn't want to be a girl, although it did explain why I was so bad at <u>football</u>.

Then suddenly I started crying. I think it was something to do with knowing that I was a boy really, so being called a girl really hurt. Anyway, as I howled like a baby Ralph called me a girl again, and the noise brought Dad rushing out of the house. He was in his underpants and hissed something about waking the neighbours and me sitting on a cushion for a week, then went back indoors.

'See,' I blubbed. 'They all pick on me.'

Ralph laughed.

'What's so funny about that?' I said. 'I'm doomed!'

'Not that,' he said. 'Your cat's just fallen off the wall.'

'That's not *my* cat,' I told him. 'It's my big sister's. Lost its tail in a cat flap, when the flap flapped back like a guillotine.' Come to think of it, that was probably when my big sister stopped liking me, because somehow the tail found itself hidden *by accident* under a lettuce leaf on her plate, and I got the blame when she nearly ate it!

14

---

'I thought the lettuce leaf might rub the tail better like a dock leaf,' I told my grim parents when they stood me on the kitchen table and demanded an explanation. 'I thought the tail might grow another body or something!'

Mel thought it was a huge hairy caterpiller and screamed the house down. It was brilliant! 'Anyway,' I said to Ralph, 'since that day, the cat has lost its sense of balance and falls off walls all the time.' This time it had fallen on our fat dog – Mr E.

Mr E is a pug dog that belonged to my granny before she died. Everyone hates him, which means that he and me have got quite a lot in common, because everyone hates me too. He's bad tempered, horribly ugly, licks blood, his breath stinks and he wipes his nose on my socks. For some unknown reason, we saved

his life. If *we* hadn't taken him after Granny's funeral, the man from the restaurant on the motorway would have chopped him up into cheeseburgers, apparently.

Suddenly there was wailing and whining outside the tent where it was dead dark and spooky. A shadow of a giant monster fell across the roof. We could see its arms and legs pressed against the canvas just like in a horror film! I screamed a high-pitched scream, and Ralph and Aaron did the same. **'Help! It's a werewolf!'** I shouted. Aaron thought it was Dracula and

Ralph thought it was a dead body that had got up and walked! 'Or that Tony Blair Witch thing!' I cried. We were so scared Aaron peed on the biscuits by accident.

AAAAAAGH

OOPS

This was a real accident. Aaron would not pee on the biscuits 'by accident', because he loves biscuits.

Then the monster put its face through the flap and the screaming stopped. It was my big brother William. He was laughing as if it was the best joke in the world. He was laughing so hard we could see his fillings. He called us *girls*!

'I'm going to get you!' I promised.

'I'd like to see you try!' he said. So I did. It wasn't that hard actually.

'Mummy! Daddy!' I shouted. 'William's being horrible to me. He's trying to scare us to death!' That was all there was to it. I heard a door slam, then my big sister poked her head through the tent flap. Her face was covered in green mud and looked really cross.

'Some of us have got a really important date tomorrow,' she growled. 'Some of us are trying to get some beauty sleep!'

'Some of us need it!' I whis-pered to Aaron, but unfortunately she heard. Now it was *her* turn to hate me.

'And who said you could have

Napoleon?' she screeched.

'No, please, Mel,' I said, clutching the cat to my chest, 'he's my hot water bottle. I'm cold.' But she snatched him out of my arms and took him back in the house just so I couldn't have him. And that was when Dad turned up for a second time, sent William to his room and glared at me. 'If this is "well-behaved", I'm a pork chop,' he growled. 'Your mother is exhausted.'

'But William was trying to murder us,' I said in my most pathetic voice.

'I don't care if he was trying to flash fry you in oil of sperm whale and force feed you to flesh-stripping locusts!' he said (which was a particularly nice thing for a father to say).

19

'You promised your mother you'd be good, Alistair. If you carry on like this she won't have you on her show. Now start behaving like a human being and let your mother get some rest!' Dad stumbled back indoors, treading in Ralph's sick as he went. When it squidged between his toes he made more noise than all of us put together!

'Can your mum get *us* on the telly?' Ralph asked.

'Oh please,' begged Aaron.

'No,' I said. 'I can go on because I'm related. You're just ordinary people. It doesn't count.'

'Bum!' sniggered Ralph. 'If your mum's a TV cook, does that mean she cooks TVs?' Then he put on silly voices and pretended to be me and my mum talking. '"What's for supper, famous mummy?" "Lovely roast aerials, Alistair."'

'No,' I said sadly, 'it means she poisons us when she tries out her new recipes.'

As we were drifting off to sleep, Aaron whispered, 'Alistair, your family really *don't* love you, do they?'

'Not much,' I sobbed softly. 'But I'll make them pay!'

Then, after a long dark pause Aaron said, 'We could be your family. Ralph and me. Just a thought. Night.'

# SUNDAY

Woke up at first light and could not believe my luck. It was like the Revenge Fairy had been. Only it wasn't a fairy, it was a revenge cat. Napoleon had brought a dead bird and a half-eaten frog into the tent and left them under my nose as a present. I don't know how it happened, but somehow *by accident* these dead things got into William and Mel's slippers while they were still sleeping!

I was downstairs having breakfast when my big sister woke up and put her toes in the frog. Her screams carried right through the floorboards. Me, Ralph and Aaron nearly choked on our cereal. But

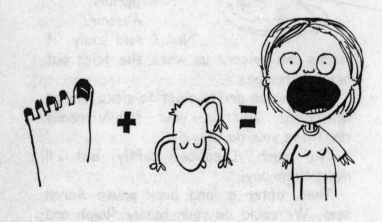

when Mel's screams woke up William and he squelched the bird and started screaming too, that was payback-tastic!

Five minutes later, Mum came downstairs carrying the squashed frog and bird in a dustpan.

'Alistair,' she said, 'did you have anything to do with this?'

'No, Mummy,' I said, innocently. 'I love my brother and sister. Besides, if I want to be a TV celebrity I have to be good, don't I? It must have been the cat!' Then while Mum went out to the dustbin, Aaron, Ralph and I burst out laughing! Unfortunately, I laughed so much I burped milk out of my nostrils and dribbled it into the marmalade. It was like having a nosebleed, only this blood was cold and had come out of a cow's

I'd like to thank everyone who's ever known me for this well-deserved Oscar!

udder. 'Mummy,' I cried when she came back in. 'I feel sick.' So Aaron and Ralph were sent home and I spent the day on the sofa wrapped in a warm blanket. Oh, poor, poor me! It did mean, however, that my big brother and sister weren't allowed to touch me!

Then Mum spoiled it all by bringing up the dreaded piano lesson with Mrs Muttley. I hate Mrs Muttley. She laughs like a hyena and shrieks so loud my eardrums bleed, but Mum's got it into her head that I'm going to be the next Charlotte Church. I have pointed out that Charlotte Church is a girl and signs, whereas I am a boy who plays the piano, but she's just thinking about the millions of pounds I could make her. In this respect, doing piano is just another form of child slavery that must be resisted. It doesn't matter that Mrs Muttley has breath like a camel and a neck like a turkey, Mum says I have to practise. But if I practise I'll get better and if I get better I'll have to have lessons for ever

and ever, and I think I'd rather eat warm horse manure!

'You've missed your last four piano lessons,' she said, 'because of too much homework.' The old 'too much homework' excuse never fails! 'So I've rearranged your next lesson for three weeks on

Sunday. And you'll be pleased to hear I've managed to book it for two and a half hours to make up for all that lost time. Ten till twelve thirty. OK?' She watched my face fall. 'You're always free on Sundays.'

'But I'm thinking of starting to play Sunday rugby with Will.'

'You've never played rugby, Alistair. You hate sport, remember?' Her lips stiffened. 'You're doing piano.'

'But I've just thought,' I said. 'What if I suddenly become religious between now and three weeks on Sunday? And what if I have a long pray on the day? My fingers might be too tired to play the piano.' Mum was prepared to take the risk.

I hate Mum. I wish Aaron and Ralph *were* my family. We could be like

the Mafia and put Mrs Muttley in a concrete overcoat, then I wouldn't have to play that stupid, monotonous *March Of The One-Legged Elephant* ever again! Sadly though, in this backward country, children are still not allowed to divorce their parents. Maybe, instead of being brothers, Aaron, Ralph and me could have a secret club. We could call it the Revengers. Members could meet to discuss interesting and varied ways to zap my big brother and sister. Torture would be allowed. But *NO* mercy!

Have just made two secret phone calls. Aaron and Ralph also think that a secret club sounds wicked! They are massively up for it and have promised to bring evil thoughts into school tomorrow. I am so happy that I have just put a new sign on my bedroom door next to my picture of Gareth Southgate and my other three signs.

> 1) IF YOU KICK ME YOU ARE ONLY
> KICKING YOURSELF!
> (Zen and the art of surviving
> big brothers and sisters)
> 2) NO MEMBER OF THE FURY
> FAMILY MAY ENTER AT ANY TIME
> UNLESS THEY SIGN A BIT OF PAPER
> FREELY ADMITTING THAT
> MASTER A. FURY ESQ. IS NOT ONLY
> A TOTAL G, BUT A Q-T TOO!
> 3) KEEP OUT - TOXIC FARTS.

The new sign says,

> BEWARE! JUDGEMENT DAY IS SOONER
> THAN YOU THINK. THE COUNTDOWN
> HAS BEGUN.

And I signed it

# The Revengers.

I can't sleep I'm so excited.

I am keeping a daily score so that I can see all the time that I am the best!

Alistair 1 - Rest of Family 0

# MONDAY

Not a good start to the day. Someone has drawn a bare bottom on my new sign in black felt tip and signed it WF. I suspect William.

Better news at breakfast. I was reading the back of the Coco Pops packet when suddenly I remembered the Spot The Ball competition that I had entered last month. This week they announce the result! And when I win I shall be famous, just like Charlotte Church, only (Mother, take note) *without* the piano.

Then things took a sharp turn for the worse again. Mum has started testing new recipes for her cookery show. I know I should say that she's the best cook in the world,* but the truth is even filthy flies won't eat her food.

*especially as I have to be nice to her to get on the telly

29

## This is a list of some of her new recipes:

*Fish eyes in goats cheese chowder*
*Polish vodka and raw beetroot soup*

yvuurk

*Bony fish pie with lentils*
*Snails tartare with sour cherry sauce*
*Maggoty pheasant and vinegar pie*
*Mashed black-eyed beancakes with*
*wildly wrinkled mushrooms*

bleeurgh

*Tooting green curry with lemongrass
rice and extra large chilli-balls*

vmmph

*Broccoli soufflé with pears
in marrowbone jelly
Prune and carrot cake with
aniseed marzipan
Liver and bacon ice-cream*

She asked us what we thought. In my head I thought *PUKE!* but out loud I said, 'Delicious!' just to be nice. Nobody else said a word.

'Thank you, Alistair,' said my mum. 'It's nice to be appreciated. You can be my official taster.' I think I may have started something I'm going to regret.

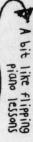

A bit like flipping piano lessons

# TOP SECRET!

First meeting of the Revengers in lunch break at school. Met in the Second Year loos where we would not be disturbed. Ralph stood at the door and kept all Second Years out. He was like a bouncer. It didn't matter how desperately boys wanted to go he just wouldn't let them in!

The Revengers have now got:

a) A secret handshake, which is so secret I've forgotten how it goes. Ralph wouldn't let us practise it in case someone was spying.

b) A secret password that a Revenger must say to another Revenger to identify himself. Anyone who doesn't know the secret password can't be a Revenger and anyone who isn't a Revenger can be killed. The secret password is 'Peanut butter and jam sandwiches'. Actually, it's more of a pass*phrase*.

c) A secret look. This look is a sort of scowl with a narrowing of the eyes. If any Revenger member sees another Revenger member doing this

Revenger look, the Revenger member knows that the Revenger member doing the Revenger look is in trouble, and the Revenger member not doing the Revenger look will immediately spring to the aid of the Revenger member doing the look. It's simple but brilliant too.

d) Invisible ink for writing invisible messages like this one:

*I love Pamela Whitby. I love Pamela Whitby. I love Pamela Whitby. I love Pamela Whitby. I love Pamela Whitby. I love Pamela Whitby.*

Nobody knows this secret. Not even Pamela Whitby. I think I'd die if anyone told her.

How quickly does this ink go invisible? I have waited one hour now and still no sign of vanishing.

2 hours – the writing's still there.

3 hours – I'm really worried that we have

Pamela Whitby must n see this diary!

been sold invisible ink that is not invisible.

We sorted out the club rules:

**1. No taking revenge out on
   another Revenger member.
2. No cowardly behaviour in the
   face of the enemy.
3. All sweets must be shared.**

Afterwards, we dreamed
up the most worst revenges
on my big brother
for being so mean
the night before
and scaring our
pants off with
the wailing ghost
thing. I thought
of piranha fish
in his bath. 'It'd
be funny if I
swapped the soap
for a piranha fish,'
I said. 'Imagine my
big brother singing in the bath. '*La la la la
la! Oh I think I'll just soap my willy now.*' He
takes the soap out of the soap dish and . . .

'*aaaaaagh!*' Lots of blood. Lots of tears, and one big brother leaps out of bath minus dangly part of his anatomy! Ha ha!'

Ralph thought of cutting William's legs off just below the knee so that he'd be forced to see the world from down where we were. 'Then he might be more nicer to people who are shorter than him,' he said. But we thought leg-chopping was going a bit too far. Breaking his knees with a base-ball bat would have been all right, but actual severance, no.

But Aaron's idea was the best. He thought of cutting the brakes on William's bike, then telling him that there were naked women at the bottom of a really steep hill and that if he cycled really fast down the really steep hill he might just see them! Ha ha! Splat!

After our meeting, when we finally left the loos, we found hundreds of Second Years hopping and fidgeting outside. It was like a Martian had landed and given them all a disease of wet trousers. Teachers stood around looking confused and not knowing why everyone was damp.

Have just eaten Mum's supper and am lying in bed next to a bucket, with sheets of newspaper on my duvet in case I'm sick again. We had fish eyes in goats cheese chowder. That's blinking soup to those who've never had it! When Mum produced it Dad left the table. 'I'm not eating that,' he said.

'Neither am I,' said William. 'I'll have toast.'

'Me too,' said Mel.

'And me!' I added.

'But I thought you were going to be my little taster,' she said. 'I thought you were going to be nice to me, Alistair, so that you could come on the telly with me.'

I wanted to be nice, but when she pushed the bowl in front of me, the whites of the eyes

36

This is just another example of the chips of the world being stacked against me like a potato mountain.

rolled over in the soup and stared deep inside me, just like William always did before he used me as a punchbag.

TONS
of
TONS ←WILL

'Shall I serve him?' sniggered William, stirring the pot.

If I was living in the future I'd have my neck changed for a spring. Then the next time William smacked me, my head would spring forward and nut him!

'Aren't *you* having any?' I said to Mum.

'No,' she replied. 'I don't like eyes.'

'BUT NEITHER DO I!' I wailed.

'Don't be so selfish,' said my big brother. 'If Mummy's gone to the trouble of cooking

it for you, you can *see* your way to eating it!' He was loving this.

'Besides,' added Mum. 'You don't know you don't like eyes until you've tried them.'

Well, now I *have* tried them, and surprise, surprise . . . I DON'T LIKE EYES!

Major planning under the bedclothes:

## Aim
to get back into Mum's good books and pay back target.

## Target
William, of course.

## Reason
For encouraging Mum to make me eat food with eyelids.

## Weapon
Chocolax – *'the laxative that keeps you going and*
*going*
*and*
*going*
*and going . . .'*

Ha ha!

The eyes have it 2-2.
But looking forward to BIG score tomorrow!

# TUESDAY

Before school I gave Mum a big kiss and said, 'Thank you for those delicious eyeballs last night, Mummy. You're such a good cook. Could we have banana splits tonight, do you think? With crumbly chocolate flakes on? Would that be OK, Mummy?'

She went all gooey-eyed and kissed me back. 'Who's a little charmer,' she said. And I turned away as if I was embarrassed, but I wasn't really. I was being dead cunning.

Before supper, while I just happened to be in the kitchen, somehow, *by accident*, the normal chocolate flakes got scraped off William's banana split and laxative chocolate got

Brilliant acting

grated on instead! When I have finished with William, he will be spending the whole night with smelly belly and it serves him right-up-his-popo!

I wanted Mum to cook something disgusting again for supper, so that William would refuse it and be really really hungry for his pudding. Then he would eat his banana split like a starving dog and not notice the funny-tasting chocolate! But what does Mum do? She only serves beef-burger and chips! It's not fair! Beefburger and chips is William's favourite – he always eats too much! By the time pudding came round he was stuffed.

'Go on,' I said, pushing my revenge across the table. 'Have a banana split.'

'Can't!' he said. 'Too full.'

'Yes you can!' I shouted. 'You have to!'

'If you want it, Alistair, just say so,' said my dad. 'I'm sure William won't mind.'

'I don't want it,' I said.

'Yes you do,' said Mum. 'You were the one who asked for banana splits this morning. Go on, Alistair, treat yourself.' How could I tell her it wasn't a treat?

'Alice,' said William smugly. 'You haven't done something naughty to my banana split, have you?'

'No,' I said, over-defensively.

'Then eat it,' he said. And I was stuffed.

In both senses of the word. ↑

It is four o'clock in the morning. It feels like my guts have just been squeezed through a mangle. Never again. I have spent the last five hours on the loo with my bottom making noises like a hippopotamus sucking a thick milkshake.

William heard me groaning, came in and laughed, and said what a shame it was that I had a bad dose of banana splats. If I had not been at death's door I would have hit him on the head with a loo brush and locked him in the bathroom with the smell. As it was, I was sitting there for so long, I read six comics and a magazine called *Top Girl*, which had a quiz in it. **BIG SISTERS – HOW MUCH DO YOU REALLY HATE YOUR LITTLE BROTHER?** Mel had filled it in and scored loads and loads! – the highest score possible. I wish I knew more about electricity, because I'd really like her door handle to somehow get wired up to the mains *by accident* and give her a huge electric shock. But I only know about insects and stuff, so I took the torch into the garden and dug up some worms, which, *by accident*, somehow got lost in her socks.

Unexpected banana bummer 2-5

Mum had to chuck a bucket of cold water over Mel this morning. She had hysterics when she put her socks on. Actually it was me who had hysterics, she just had a screaming fit. It was the funniest thing I'd ever seen! That was when the phone rang.

My prayers have been answered! I am really close to being famous and wearing dark glasses all the time! The woman on the phone said that I have reached the last six in the Coco Pops Spot The Ball FA Cup Challenge. If I win I will get a phone call in a week's time telling me how to collect my prize – three tickets to the FA Cup Final! I will take Aaron and Ralph. Between you and me, Diary, I only entered the competition to annoy William. I hate football, but he worships it, so if I win I shall go without him and really upset him. Seeing William seething with envy is definitely worth ninety boring minutes of my time!

When I got off the phone Mum asked me it I'd lost weight. She thought I looked thinner than last night. I told her I'd been banana-ed and did indeed feel a little drained. She told me to go back to bed, which was good in one way, but bad in two others, because Mum brought me a left-over bowl of goats cheese chowder with fish eyes in, and after her worm trauma, Mel was allowed to stay off school too.

She pushed notes under my bedroom door all day, calling me a poisonous little toad and threatening to get her Luke to break my legs. So I ran downstairs shouting, 'Mummy! Mel's calling me horrible names!'

And Mel charged in after me shouting, 'Well it's his fault! He knows I hate wriggly things. Tell him, Mummy. Tell him that if he does it again I'm allowed to kill him and you won't mind.' My mum was up to her elbows in stuffed prunes and said, 'Whatever, darling.' Which shows you in one sentence what a cruel and evil mother she can be.

I told my dad what Mel had said when he came home early before lunch. He's the boss at the local leisure centre. They'd just got a new television for the gym and he'd brought it home to try it out. He was lying on the sofa watching golf.

'Fetch us a beer, Alistair.'

'Is what you're doing really work?' I asked.

'Oh yes,' he said. 'Highly skilled. And some crisps.'

'Did you know that Mum said Mel could kill me today?' I told him.

To which my dad replied, 'Golf buggies are brilliant though, aren't they? If I played golf I wouldn't walk anywhere. I'd have a chauffeur to drive me.' What was the point?

If I disappeared off the face of the earth tomorrow would I be missed? Would my family weep and wail and tear their hair out? Or would they have a nice lunch and watch the golf?*

When William came home I was watching cartoons and sitting in the comfy armchair. He up-ended the chair, shook me out and turned over to women's football.

'But you don't like women's football,' I protested.

'No, but neither do you, and that's the most important thing,' he smirked.

'Dad!' I moaned. 'Dad! Dad! Dad!' But Dad was asleep, so somehow I slipped and *by accident* punched his leg. 'Dad, William's just thrown me out of the armchair. *And* he's just turned over and I was watching!'

'Fried egg, double bubble and beans,' said Dad. He was sleep-talking.

'Anyway,' I said to William, wheeling out my big gun. 'I'm probably going to the FA Cup Final with Ralph and Aaron.'

'What?' he gasped. 'How?'

'They're phoning me next week to tell me if I've won the tickets.'

'Oh, but that's not fair!' he whined. 'You know I love football more than you.'

'Really?' I said. 'If only I'd known.' I was making out like that was the first I'd ever heard of it.

47

'And I've *always* wanted to see the FA Cup Final,' he said. By now I was smirking. 'Why are you taking Aaron and Ralph instead of me? I'm your brother.'

'Because Aaron and Ralph are my friends,' I said. 'I like them!'

Then Mel came in to watch MTV, but there was a snake in a video so she screamed and ran upstairs to phone her boyfriend instead.

Supper was bony fish pie with lentils and I was sick. While I had my head down the loo, Mum started crying because none of her family liked her food. Her 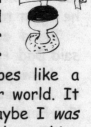 sobs echoed up the pipes like a ghostly wail from another world. It crossed my mind that maybe I *was* dead. There was certainly nothing left inside me. I was like an Egyptian mummy – perfect on the outside but empty within.

Before I went to sleep, Dad came up to see me. He was wearing his cheesy face, like a holy vicar who has something deep and meaningful to say.

'Just wanted a word,' he said thought-fully. 'Your mother and I were hoping that your behaviour might improve, Alistair, if we promised you could appear on the telly. But it hasn't, has it? It's got worse.'

I wanted to explain that it wasn't my fault. That William and Mel were always the ones who started it. That I was only ever the victim. But I knew he wouldn't believe me. So instead, I said nothing and put on a face that looked like I was inter-ested in what he was saying. He sat down on the edge of the bed and I knew I was in for a serious man to man chat. Dad's chats are famous. He thinks we'll remember them for the rest of our lives and pass his wisdom on to our children, but I wouldn't be so cruel.

'Son,' he said, 'life is a bit like a game of tug and war.'

'Tug *of* war,' I said.

blah blah blah blah blah blah blah blah blah blah

DAD
The Wisdom of Mr Fury

'That's what I said,' he said, 'tug and war . . . in which he who pulls the hardest often does not win. Whereas he who tugs just a little bit at a time often edges it.'

'But that's not true,' I said. 'If I gave one huge tug while you were giving little tiny ones I'd pull you over.'

'It's a saying, Alistair. I'm not saying it's always right. It's just something to think about.'

'I shall learn it by heart,' I said.

'So can I tell your mum you're going to keep her food down from now on?'

'I'll inform my stomach,' I said.

'Good. And practise your piano?'

'Just about to do some,' I lied sweetly.

Dad took a deep breath. 'It's just that whenever there's trouble at home, Alistair, you're always there.'

'That's because I live there,' I said.

pooft

50

*and have been on telly with Mum, obviously

## KNOW THIS PARENTS!

When I can swim and have conquered my fear of sharks, and can build a shelter, and fly a small plane, and eat coconuts and berries, and have bought myself a pair of flip flops to walk on hot sand,* I am moving to a desert island with only *one* phone and *not* giving my family the number!

KEEP OUT

Win some, lose some, sick some up 5-6

51

# THURSDAY

Woke up in a bad mood. I think it's hunger. I haven't eaten proper food for two days. Went back to school with a note from Mum and immediately got into trouble. Miss Bird, my form teacher, wanted to know why I hadn't done my History homework – collecting information about my ancestors for a family tree.

'I've been ill,' I said. 'I had food poisoning.'

'That's a lie,' she said. 'Your mother's note says you've been "under the weather". "Under the weather" is no excuse for not doing your homework, Fury. You have till Wednesday or it's a detention!' This was a bad day getting worse! I hated Mum for not owning up to being a poisoner and I hated Miss Bird for always giving me detentions and lines and extra work for no reason.

STOP THIS TORTURE

## This is Miss Bird:

We call her Pigeon because she's got a beaky nose and waddles when she walks like she's got a fifty-pence piece clenched between her buttocks.

Pamela Whitby says Miss Bird takes it out on me, because she teaches cooking and hates my mum for making money out of

rubbish recipes that she could cook with her eyes closed. But when you think about it, if Miss Bird cooks with her eyes closed, that's exactly why my mum's a famous cook and Miss Bird will never be anything but a scummy teacher with a squint. One day I'll tell her that.

Was very polite to Mum when I got home. With my TV celebrity status at stake, I did not want to upset her again. 'Just off to practise my piano,' I said. Then, 'Oh by the way, why did you not write "food poisoning" in my note?'

'Because I did not poison you,' she said.

'I think you did,' I said. 'Twice.'

'Not deliberately.' Mum was blushing. 'Besides, before I put

---

my recipes in a book, I've got to make sure they're fit for human consumption.'

Gasp! Horror! It's a sad day when you discover that your own mother is using you as a guinea pig! 'Aren't I human too?' I cried, choking back bitter tears of rejection. 'If the food's *not* fit to eat you'll kill me first!'

'You're not human,' interrupted Mel. 'You're an evil swamp monster with the mind of a lavatory bowl!' That does it! The gloves are off. Nobody calls me a swamp monster and lives to tell the whole family again and again at every Sunday lunch from now till Christmas. Mel deserves everything the Revengers can throw at her!

And I'm not practising Mrs Muttley's stupid piano either!

WANTED

For crimes against A. Fury, the beauty industry and the human race.
THE REVENGERS

55

Napoleon has done a bunk. Nobody's seen him for a couple of days and Mel blames me. I know she doesn't care really. She hates that cat, but loves any chance of getting me into trouble. Only now it's not just me, is it? Because now I have the power that comes from being a Revenger!

Had the second secret meeting of the Revengers at break, and, based on the phobia of the target, came up with an absolutely brilliant evil secret revenge plan.

14 pairs of wet trousers this time!

Obviously, I can't tell you who the target of this brilliant evil secret revenge plan is in case my big sister reads this diary, but I *can* say that it's payback for everything bad she's ever done or said to me, and rats are only *part* of the surprise! It's going to be brilliant and secret. And evil of course.

Actually between you and me, Diary, I'm rather nervous. Accidentally torturing Mel with a snake was Ralph's idea after I'd made the mistake of saying that she didn't like them. But I don't think I want a snake. They're cold and dangerous, especially if they wriggle up your trousers. And if they get into your bedroom, they use your face as a pillow apparently. But Ralph told me it was the only way to give Mel what was coming to her and Aaron agreed. So I lost.

Napoleon is still at large. Mum says that if he's not back by tomorrow we're going to have to start a search with tree posters and everything. Dad says we should search the Island of Elba because Napoleon will probably be there, but I don't know where that is and anyway I don't plan to do any searching at all. He's not *my* hot-water bottle.

A good Revenger never forgets!

57

I placed an anonymous advert in *Loot*:

WANTED –
GLASS TANK
AND RAT CAGE –
CONTACT
THE REVENGERS

and paid for it with Dad's credit card. When the lady on the other end of the phone asked me if I was old enough to have a credit card, I told her I was forty-four.

'I only sound like I'm eleven, because I'm the product of a horrible scientific experiment. Years ago, they tried to make a human fly by stitching the wings of a bat onto a boy. That was me. I've still got the wings, but now I've got a squeaky voice too.'

'Is the cage for you?' asked the lady.

'Can't answer that now,' I said, 'I really must hang upside down from the ceiling. Bye.'

I needed at least £30 to buy the tank and cage, and the snake as well, and the food too, because snakes love live rats apparently. Make that £60.

Asked parents what they'd most like to see me do with my life. Dad said play for England. Mum said play piano at the Albert Hall. I said I'd do both if they paid me to practise, but they refused. So I asked for jobs around the house. Suggested that bed making and room tidying were worth at least £5 each per day.

'I'm not paying you to make your own bed,' said Dad. 'You should be doing that anyway.'

'Like brushing your teeth,' said Mum.

'All right,' I said. 'How about I refuse to

brush my teeth unless you give me money?'

'That's blackmail,' he said.

'Yes,' I said. 'What's wrong with that?' I also had another brilliant idea, that they could pay me for *not* picking my nose and *not* leaving my flies undone! They said they'd see what they could find for me to do, but only if I told them what I wanted the money for.

↑ Never seen a mouth

'A pet,' I said.

'You've got Mr E and Napoleon,' they said.

'A normal pet,' I said.

'Like what?'

'A crocodile!' I said.

'No!' they screamed.

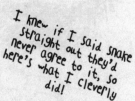

I knew if I said snake straight out they'd never agree to it, so here's what I cleverly did!

'OK, a vulture,' I said.
**'No!'** they yelled.

'How about a snake then?'
'Oh all right, but only a little one?'

Size doesn't matter where Mel's concerned! Me 8- Them 6

Dad said he was thinking of building an extension to the kitchen and was I interested in doing the work?

'Will I have to climb a ladder?' I asked. Dad said I would, so I said I'd do it, because climbing ladders is fun. 'But I'll need a book, or something, to copy,' I said. 'I've never built an extension before.'

'Haven't you?' laughed Dad. 'You'll pick it up.'

'And how much will you pay me?' I asked.

'Six thousand pounds,' he said, 'but I want it done by lunchtime.' And he walked away. I stood there all morning waiting for

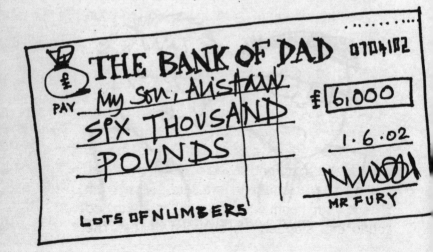

THE BANK OF DAD 0704102

PAY My son, Alistair £ 6,000

SIX THOUSAND

POUNDS                              1.6.02

                                    MR FURY

LOTS OF NUMBERS

him to come back, but he never did. Sadly I don't know what an extension looks like or I could have made a start – or maybe even finished it, which would have been good. As it is, I am now £6,000 short.

No lunch today, because big sisters and parents were having a huge row over Luke. He's asked her to a weekend party in the middle of her exams, and Mel's said yes without asking Mum and Dad.

'I'm sixteen!' she yelled. 'I'm old enough to marry him. You can't stop me!'

'I thought it was just a party,' said Dad. 'Where did the dreaded "M" word spring from?'

'You're not going,' said Mum. '*After* your exams, that's fine, but not *during*!'

'But I love him!' wailed Mel.

'Good, then he won't mind waiting a few days,' said Mum.

'That's not fair!' screamed my big sister, kicking a chair across the floor. 'It's *my* life!' Then she stormed out, shouting, 'I wish I was dead and living somewhere else!'

And when I cheered and said, 'Great! Can I have your room when you go?' she turned round and slapped me so hard across the

Be VERY careful

*I mean *nearly* cried. I didn't actually cry, obviously, because I don't cry. Well, I did once, when I caught my winky in a zip, but that's all right, because that's a man thing!

---

ear that I heard bells and wind, like I was sitting with goats on the side of a mountain.

And when I cried,* Mum said, 'Serves you right, you little troublemaker!' Huh! And there was innocent-little-me thinking it was Mel who was causing all the trouble!

Sometimes I think, in the history of mankind, that there has only ever been one person who was worse off than me, apart from the Elephant Man obviously, and

Gareth Southgate when he missed that penalty,* and that is the Queen's horse for having her big bottom sitting on him all the time, and Chips from the *Dandy*.

The 'clip-round-the-ear-from-Mel' incident has had two effects. 1) She's really asked for it this time. 2) It has brought my frail mind under control. I no longer fear snakes. Bring on the Boa of Revenge!

* Sorry. That's t .

Today, I am the slapped, but tomorrow I will be the slapper! 8-8

# SUNDAY

Hoovered the stairs = 50p.

Washed the bath = 20p.

Walked the dog = 75p.

Made posters for Lost

Cat = 1p each.

It is not enough. Revenge,
however sweet, does not
come cheap.

Granny Constance came to lunch. She
was impressed with the way I cleared the
table and did the washing up, but was
shocked to find out that I was only doing it
for hard cash. I took her for a walk in the
park and showed her the ducks.

'They're extra,' I said.

'Whatever do you mean?' she asked.

'Nothing,' I smiled. But when I got home I
charged Mum £1.50 for the walk and added
on a surcharge of 25p for 'brightening

Granny's day with pond life'. Then I washed the car, polished the silver, weeded the front path, unloaded the dishwasher, wiped the finger-plates, picked up rubbish and combed the cat and dog with Mum's hair-brush.

It is the end of the working day and I have earned a mighty £11.35, but at what cost to my health? I am exhausted. I am more wrung out than a flannel. In the name of revenge, I have slaved for nearly two WHOLE HOURS today! But remember, I am *more* tired than a slave would be, because I haven't stopped for tea and biscuits or anything!

'Piano practise?' asked Mum.

'Too tired!'

Dad just came in and asked if I was still trying to earn money to buy a tank and a rat cage. I told him I was. 'Like the ones we've got in the attic?' he asked. I could not believe it! He'd had them in the attic all along. All that work for nothing!

'You might have said!' I said.

'Yes, but if I had,' he smiled, 'you wouldn't have done all those chores for me, would you?'

I feel used. Own goal 1-9

I don't even know who's playing in the FA Cup Final, and quite frankly I don't give a monkey's. Winning the tickets and *not* giving one to William is all I care about! He's tried to be nice to me twice now, but he's *not* coming!

Must keep this secret from Dad. If he finds out he's bound to take William's side and make me give him a ticket. Sometimes I wonder if Dad is my real dad at all – after all, he loves sport and I don't. And he always wants me to change who I am, as if who I am isn't good enough. Maybe I'm different, because I *am* different. Sets you thinking.*

After school, Ralph, Aaron and I went to the pet shop and bought a boa constrictor called Alfred. He cost £12, which was cheaper than I was expecting, but snakes are sold by the metre and Alfred is only twenty-two centimetres long. The man in the shop says he'll grow to three metres. When he asked if

Sometimes I am awash with maturity

I wanted any food, I said I didn't have enough money and would have to come back for some rats when I did. So the nice man gave me two frozen mice to keep the wolf from Alfred's door.

My name is REVENGE

I cycled home with Alfred in my ruck-sack and slipped him into one of William's rugby socks. Then I tied up the top so he couldn't get out, tiptoed into my big sister's room and put the sock under her duvet with a note attached: MY NAME IS REVENGE.

At supper I could hardly contain myself. I was so full of nervous anticipation that I ate two helpings of snails tartare thinking it was pasta. My mum called me her little angel and I let her give me a big hug. It was the perfect moment to ask the question I'd been dying to ask for weeks. 'Have you spoken to Michael yet?' I asked, 'about me being on the telly?' Michael was Mum's TV producer.

'I will,' she said. 'I definitely heard her say, 'I will.'

Went to bed early and lay in the dark waiting for big sister to come upstairs. I heard her feet climbing. Then I heard shuffling, followed by rustling, screaming, crying, running, stamping, howling, sobbing, thumping and more screaming!

I ran onto the landing where Mel was dancing naked round an empty sock. She

69

was throwing her clothes off, shouting, 'Is it on me? Is it on me?'

By now Mum and Dad were up the stairs

and William was trying to take photos of Mel to sell to his mates at school, and I was standing there like a little angel, going, 'What is the matter, Mel? Have you seen a ghost?' But under my breath I was snickering, because I knew what I'd done!

'Who put the snake in Melanie's bed?' That was Mum. She sounded stressed.

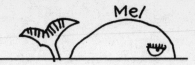

'Was it you, Alistair?'

'No,' I said. But then I remembered that I'd told them I wanted to buy one so I changed my tune. 'I mean, yes, Mummy. I thought Mel liked snakes. I was sharing my new pet with her. Was that not a nice thing to do?'

'You know snakes make my flesh crawl!' shuddered Mel.

'No, I didn't know that,' I said sweetly. 'It's only a *little* baby boa constrictor. It's lovely really. Would you like to see it eat a mouse?' Mel screamed again. 'Oh, that reminds me. Has anyone found Napoleon, because this snake could easily gobble him up by accident!'

'Stop it, Alistair!' shouted Mum. But Henry VIII didn't stop chopping off his wives' heads just because his mum told him

71

Encore!

More!

BRAVO!!!

The boy is a GENIUS!

to. It was too much fun.

'Don't be such a girl,' I grinned. 'It's not nasty. It's natural. Besides, you can hardly hear the crack of the mouse's skull as it's crushed by the snake's jaws. And you won't see much blood at all. Unless the snake's sick, of course. Then you'll see everything – heart, liver, lungs, brain . . .'

I was sent to my room.

23.25 – It's 2 hours later and I still feel brilliant!

Result! 100-9

# TUESDAY

Woke remembering poxy History homework, but refuse to let it spoil last night's brilliant victory. I shall ask Mum and Dad about their ancestors tonight.

Outside the bathroom I had the power over Melanie, who couldn't look me in the eye. She was still upset, because now she thought my snake had eaten her cat! She was crying when she told me to help look for Napoleon.

'Go on,' said Mum. 'Do something useful for once, Alistair.'

'I can't,' I said. 'I've got to practise my piano.' Then to my mother's astonishment I went back into my bedroom and ran my finger up the keyboard, but half the keys were sticking and when I thumped middle C there was a loud squelch.

I have one tiny problem. Now that revenge is done and the joke is over, I am left with a snake. As I explained to Ralph at the second secret meeting, I don't like

snakes and haven't the foggiest how to look after them. Do I have to clean out the tank? Do I have to scoop up its poop in a plastic bag? I don't even know if it does poop. It could be pellets or guacamole, like iguanas do. And how do I feed it? Do I just drop the frozen mice into the cage and let the snake do the rest, or do I have to cut the mice up and cook them with onions and salad and dollops of tomato ketchup? And what about exercise? Do I put the snake on a lead and take it for a walk with Mr E? Too many questions and not enough answers.

Because he is not the most popular guest we've ever had in our house, I shall take Alfred to school today and hope he likes noise and lots of people.

No idea

I hid him in my rucksack and sat him on the draining board all through breakfast without anyone knowing! Not even Mum's producer, Michael, knew when he arrived for a meeting. He sat down right in front of Alfred and didn't have a clue he was there, and Michael's supposed to be in TV where everyone is always looking out for funny pets to put on programmes. So he can't be very good at his job.

Apparently, Mum's first programme is going out in ten days time and the BBC are worried because they haven't seen what's in it yet. Mum's bottom lip trembled as she told Michael that she had been trying to get her recipes together, but she'd had problems.

'Really?' I said. 'What are they?' I didn't realize parents had problems. I thought all problems stopped when your big brother and sister left home. She meant *me*. 'I beg your pardon?' I said. '*I'm* the problem?' And when I casually asked Mum if Michael knew that I was going to be her helper this series, she told me to shut up.

'Celia darling, the bottom line is this,' said Michael. 'We *must* record the programme by Friday week or we won't hit transmission. And no transmission means no series.'

Mum nodded. 'Michael,' she said, 'my recipes will be ready even if it kills me.'

'Or *me*,' I said jokingly, but nobody laughed.

That was when Michael took a great big sniff and asked Mum what was cooking that smelled so delicious. She said she didn't know.

'Mice,' I said. 'I decided to cook them.' The microwave pinged and I took out two piping hot pink mice on a plate.

76

'Tell me they're marzipan!' squeaked Michael.

'No, they're mice,' I said.

'And you eat them?'

'Eat them!' I said. 'What do you think I am? They're for my snake.'

I could not have had any idea what was going to happen next.

Alfred smelled the mice and wriggled out the top of my rucksack. Then thinking Michael's blond hair was a delicious guinea pig the boa constrictor wrapped its coils around his head. Michael screamed and sprang up from the table, but this just made Alfred squeeze harder, and the harder Alfred squeezed the higher Michael's hair rose off his scalp revealing a bald head underneath. Then suddenly the hair pinged off like an elastic band and flopped into a saucepan. 'Oh it's a wig!' I cried. And with that comment I lost all chance of Mum asking Michael to make me a TV star. I knew

that, because ten seconds later she threw me and the snake out of the house.

At school, the snake caused even more chaos. I was only showing Ralph and Aaron how its constricting coils could fire globs of toothpaste out of a tube when the girls came in from the playground. They shrieked, tucked their skirts into their knickers and jumped on top of their desks. It has to be said, Pamela Whitby looked easily the most gorgeous, until she fainted and knocked a tooth out.

Panos Papayoti, who's huge and incredibly hairy for eleven, and knows all sorts of rude stuff that none of us understands, winked and said, "If you think that tucking your skirts into your knickers is going to save you from the snake, girls, think again!" Nobody knew what he was talking about.

Then Pigeon came in and a glob of toothpaste hit her right on the tip of her beak. She flapped her wings and dragged me to the front. "What is the meaning of this?" she squawked, slapping Alfred on the head. "And don't tell me it's a snake, because I hate snakes".

"Oh it's not a snake", I lied. "It's a legless, long-tailed lizard!"

*A classic detention moment if ever I'd heard one!

'It is a snake!'

cried the girls, at which Pigeon hopped on top of the desks to join them.

'Alistair Fury!'

she shouted.*

'Have five gold stars for bringing in your pet and now take it home!'

'What?' I was confused. Pigeon was being nice. 'But I'm not allowed to leave till the end of school, miss,' I said.

'Take ten goldstars!'

she shrieked.

'Don't you want to stroke it?'

'No!'

she said

# 'Make it fifteen!'

'Or watch it dislocate its jaw?'

☆

# 'How many gold stars do you want to remove that revolting reptile from my classroom?'

That was when I realized she was scared.

'Twenty,' I said. I never got gold stars and twenty was more than most people got in a term.

My joy at being the best-behaved boy in the class meant that I went home feeling ten metres tall. All I wanted was to show off my gold stars to my family and use them to bribe my way back onto Mum's TV show, but when I rushed into the hall, my big brother and sister slammed the sitting-room door in my face, and my own mother made it perfectly clear that I was less important to her than a snail soufflé.

'Go away, Alexander. I'm trying to cook!'

My name is Alistair! Not Alexander. Not Alice. ALISTAIR.

**A** for 'Ard-done-by

**L** for last

**I** for Ignored

**S** for Sweet-as-sugar-pie

**T** for Terminator

**A** for Animal handler

**I** for Innocent

**R** for

# REVENGE

---

Nobody is talking to me. I have been cast out into the wilderness and it's all Alfred's fault!

'This is the last time any of your family will speak to you,' said Mel, pinning my shoulder to the wall, 'until you apologize for being so heartless and cruel to me, and promise that your snake will never – that's NEVER – leave your room, unless of course it's dead.' Then she added. 'And it looks like *I'm* helping Mum on the telly now, because you can't behave.'

What had seemed like a brilliant idea yesterday, now seemed triple pants!

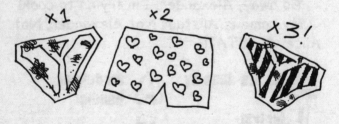

Not only that but to do my History homework I have to talk to Mum and Dad about their ancestors. But I can't talk to them if they won't talk to me. I'm going to get a detention and that's Alfred's fault too!

Later, when the phone rang, William

answered it and said, 'Alistair? No I'm afraid he's not in. Bye.'

It was too much. I burst out of my bedroom. 'Who was it?' I yelled. 'Was it the Coco Pops Challenge? Have I won?' But William said nothing. I banged on his bedroom door. 'William,' I screamed, 'you have to tell me. Who was it?'

My dad came out of the sitting room. 'What's going on, Alistair?' he said.

'Sssssh!' hissed Mel, clamping her hand over Dad's mouth. 'No talking! He's been sent to Coventry. Now go back inside and

forget you've got a younger son!' Then she pushed him through the door and stuck her tongue out at me.

And even later still, I heard footsteps pad across my bedroom floor. As I rolled over in bed a hand slipped over my mouth.

'Weurreugh?' I said.

It was Mum and Dad looking nervous. 'William and Mel must never know that we've been in here tonight?' hissed Dad. 'This conversation never happened,' added Mum, checking over her shoulder. 'We're still not talkling to you Alistair. Understood?' Dad wiped his lips and stared me in the eye. 'We're just here to say, get rid of that snake or...' He stopped.

'Or nothing', said Mum, looking crossly at him. 'Just get rid of that snake. And don't ask us to do it, because we're too scared, all right!'

It is eleven o'clock. I can't sleep. I can hear William singing to himself next door. 'I'm going to see the cup! I'm going to see the cup! E-I-addio, I've got three tickets to see the cup!' What does he mean?

# WEDNESDAY

At breakfast, I begged my big brother to tell me if I'd won the tickets, but he wouldn't talk. He just smiled and sealed his lips with an imaginary zip.

'You're lying,' I said. 'You're winding me up. I can tell.' But I couldn't really. I didn't have a clue what the truth was. I can't take much more of this silence! It is torture. If it goes on any longer I shall have to call the RSPCA and report my family for child cruelty.

It struck me on the way to school that maybe the school might like to have Alfred as an interesting specimen for the Biology labs, but when I mentioned it to Pigeon, she threw a black-board rubber at my head, burst into tears

and erupted in huge white goosebumps. She didn't look like a pigeon any more. She looked like a turkey.

'Shall I take that as a no then?' I said. As she tried to say yes a bubble of snot blew up out of her nose like bubblegum.

When Pigeon had composed herself with sweet tea, she chose me out of the whole class to stand up and talk about my family's ancestors.

Why does that always happen? If I've

*done* the homework I'm *never* asked! I don't know anything about my family except that somewhere down the line I must have been related to the Invisible Man, which explains why nobody ever notices me! So I made something up instead.

'My family is all descended from apes,' I said. 'Except Melanie and William who *are* apes!' Sometimes I think I'm a genius. Pigeon didn't think so though. I got that detention. Thank you, Alfred.

After detention, I took the snake back to the pet shop and tried to give him back. 'It's damaged goods,' I said. 'It's faulty. It's not like a normal pet, it keeps upsetting people.' But that was not the shopkeeper's problem apparently. He opened the door to the street. 'If it was a toaster you'd replace it,' I said as he patted me on the head and ushered me out. 'It's past its sell-by date!' The door shut and Alfred and I found ourselves out on the pavement.

I hate this stupid scoring thing. It's meant to show that I'm brilliant, but how can it with this stupid snake that won't go away? Me 100- Them 99 Still ahead by a rat's whisker, but only just!

More silence. No breakfast. Mel and William deliberately finished all the bread, milk and cereal before I came down. When I looked in the fridge it was full of Mum's TV food.

'What's this?' I asked Dad, picking up a green ring doughnut. 'Can I eat it?'

'It's toad in the hole,' he said. 'I wouldn't.'

'Shut up!' shouted Mel. 'Dad, you're useless. How will snake-boy ever learn his lesson if you keep talking to him?'

I definitely wish I'd never bought Alfred now. He was fun for ten minutes, but since then he's made my life a misery. If I ever want to hear the sound of a kindly human voice again that snake has got to go. But how?

And William won't stop smirking.

'We'll help you get rid of him,' said Ralph. 'Permanently.'

'You mean bump William off for good?' I said. 'It's not allowed, is it?'

'Not William, Alfred,' said Ralph. 'Wrap him up in brown paper and string, and post him to the Outer Hebrides.'

'He won't fit through the slot in the post box,' I said.

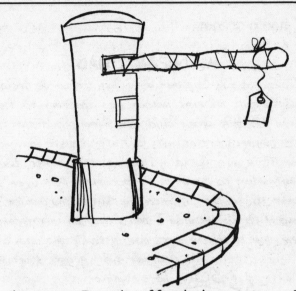

'Anyway, I can't afford the postage. I can't even afford to feed him.'

'Then *don't* feed him,' said Aaron. 'And when he dies and goes stiff, you can use him as a snooker cue!' I told them I felt like a murderer just talking about it, but they said that some murders were OK if nobody found out. I agreed to meet after school tomorrow to eliminate 'The Problem'.*

'But bring a sock,' I said.

'Why?' asked Aaron.

'As a hood. If I have to look at his inno-cent little eyes I won't be able to bash his brains out, will I!' Tomorrow it will all be over and I can get back to winning ways. 101·100

89

# FRIDAY

I had a dream.

## MY DREAM I HAD

I won the FA Cup last night, but the whole crowd was silent, because nobody was speaking to me. Even my dad, who should have been proud that I was playing sport at last, just stood there with his hands in his pockets, looking the other way, pretending to count the floodlights. And when I went to get the cup from the Queen she wouldn't give it to me, because I was wicked to animals, and she gave it to the next man instead, who was, of course, that great sporting hero, William.

The Revengers met secretly in my bedroom. I put a sign on the door to keep my family out:

We were not disturbed.

I put the sock over Alfred's head and bent a cotton bud into a U shape to make him a pair of ear-muffs. This stopped 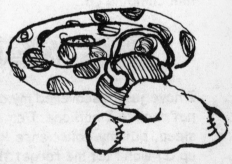 him from freaking out while we ran through all the ways of murdering a snake we could think of. Shooting, stabbing, knotting, wringing, stretching, skinning, cooking, grating, chopping, slicing . . . it got quite gruesome, actually. Ralph suggested we did something where we didn't need to be there, like burying Alfred in the garden and blowing him up with dynamite, but I put my foot down.

'If we damage Mum's flowers she'll kill us!' I said.

In the end we just dumped him in the dustbin and put a brick on the lid to stop him climbing out.

# BIG NEWS!

I have just discovered my conscience. I did not realize I had one. I am trying to get to sleep, but my conscience keeps waking me up. It won't let me forget the pathetic look on Alfred's face as I shut the dustbin lid. I wonder if Hell is as hot as everyone says it is? I shall buy sandals just in case.

Murderers are not worthy of points. 101-100

# SATURDAY

Saved! Woke this morning and my conscience has gone again! I don't feel even slightly guilty about Alfred any more. In fact I've already forgotten what he looked like, which means I can't have loved him that much. The dastardly deed is done. I am free once again!

I rushed downstairs anxious to share my glorious news. I found Dad ironing his underpants in the kitchen.

'Dad!' I cried. 'I've done what everyone wanted! You can speak to me again!' But he was having trouble with his creases and growled at me. So I told Mel and William instead.

'He's just saying he's got rid of the snake to make us like him,' my big sister said to my big brother, making sure I could hear even though she wasn't talking to me. 'Well it won't work.'

'Mum!' I shouted, rushing into the dining room where she and Michael were tasting witchetty grubs au gratin. He was wearing a pink baseball cap in case the snake fell in love with his wig again. 'Mum! You can speak to me again, I've binned the sn—'

## 'OUT!'

Something has snapped in my head. I am how officially bored of being ignored. I've tried to be good. I've disposed of the snake. I've changed! But nothing's ever good enough for my family. If I was an orphan I'd get more love and attention, but I'm not, I'm just a poor, wronged child who needs nurturing! Well, if they want war, they can have war! I *will* be noticed again.

To do this, I need to make myself the centre of attention. Here's a list of ways I could do it.

1) Pack a bag and leave home, after turning off the fridge while it's full of Mum's food.

2) Build a cat-sized coffin containing all of Napoleon's favourite things – a tin of cat food, a ball with a bell in it, a dead mouse and a picture of his tail – and give it to Mel with my love.

3) Paint a message on a sheet – HELP ME. MY PARENTS ARE ALIENS. THEY ARE GOING TO EAT ME! – and hang it out of the window.

Help! my parents are aliens!

4) Pee in my big sister's bath.

5) Hide under my bed for a week and send hostage notes to my parents, saying things like, 'Pay up now or the boy loses a whole leg!' Mind you, if I was hiding under my bed, how would I get out to post the hostage notes? And what if they didn't pay and I really did have to cut off my own leg?  Bad idea.

6) Alfred. Of course! Snakes alive! And the brilliance of this plan is I don't need to get Alfred back to do it!

I ran downstairs and burst into the dining room.

'Help!' I shouted. 'Help, the snake's escaped!' Michael leapt onto the table and screamed. Mum joined him. My big brother and sister rushed down from upstairs and my dad zipped in from the kitchen.

'What do you mean?' they shouted. 'You said you'd already got rid of the snake.'

'Lies!' I cried. 'All lies! I was covering up

for the fact that this morning the snake had grown! It was huge, far too big for the tank. I had to put my wardrobe on top of the lid to keep it in, but it must have muscled its way out – it's bigger than the Loch Ness Monster, honest it is – and slithered between the floorboards, because I can't find it. And it hasn't eaten for days so it's probably really really hungry. It could probably even eat a human! It could! And it's gone! Help! Everyone run!'

It worked.

Michael drove off so fast that his wig blew out the sunroof. Dad scooted off to his mum's where he said he'd left his glasses by mistake. My big, brave, hard-as-nails brother tried to be cool. He hung around long enough to give me a dead leg, but after that he bolted out the house saying he'd just remembered a twenty-four hour rave he had to go to. Mum ran to a wine bar, and Mel – big, sulky, I'm-the-

most-desirable-thing-on-the-planet Mel –
leapt upstairs wailing. 'That's it! I'm leaving
this slimy reptile-house. I'm going to live
with my boyfriend. Don't try to stop me!'
Nobody was trying to do anything, because
nobody was there. Then she phoned her
boyfriend and told him she was moving in
with him and his parents.

Luke the Puke

While they were on the
phone being sweethearts I
picked up the extension and
made a fart noise down the
receiver. Then I put on a high voice and
pretended to be my big sister. 'Oooh, sorry,

boyfriend Lukey darling, but I've got terrible farts since I had them beans for breakfast!' I was still laughing when Mel stormed down the stairs with a suitcase, pulled my hair and slammed out the front door. It was only when I stopped laughing that I realized my plan had been a miserable failure. How could I be the centre of attention when I was the only one in the house?

The Revengers came round. We ate something greasy with mushrooms from the fridge and discussed my problem.

'You do realize Alfred has to be found now, don't you?' said Ralph.

'Why?' I said.

'Because if your family thinks there's an uncaptured snake in the house they'll send you to Coventry for the rest of your life.' That meant we had to get him out of the dustbin and hide him somewhere where they'd find him!

Alfred looked well cross when we lifted the lid and picked him out of the dustbin with Dad's barbecue tongs.

'He could kill us,' said Aaron. 'And there's not a court in the land would convict him after what we've put him through.'

It was quite frightening hearing Alfred hiss and watching him twist his tail, but we got him into the kitchen and dropped him into a mixing bowl. Then we rolled him in pastry, lightly dusted him with flour and popped him into the fridge next to the other rolls of pastry that Mum had prepared for her television programme.

'We've got to think,' I said. 'Why would

he crawl into the fridge?' I needed a good answer in case I was asked.

'To hibernate,' said Aaron. 'They've got cold blood.'

'So why did he roll himself in pastry first?'

'Camouflage,' said Ralph. 'To hide amongst the pies!' So that was that. I'd covered my tracks. The snake had escaped and I *'did not know where it was'!*

Although I *did obviously!*

# SUNDAY

Everyone came home eventually last night, except my big sister. I've said sorry so many times I've forgotten the meaning of the word, but it seems to have done the trick. I don't think I'm in Coventry any more. I think I'm back in Tooting.

Trouble with that was this:

'Alistair.' This is the first thing my mum said to me after my punishment was over. 'There's only one week to go before your two-and-a-half-hour piano lesson with Mrs Muttley, and I haven't heard you practise once.'

'Oh, but I have,' I said. 'I practise all the time when you're out of the house, and sometimes when you're in. But the pieces I'm playing are ever so soft – so soft that sometimes even I can't hear them myself. You've heard of pianissimo, well these pieces are silencissimo. It's very very hard.'

How many bits of brilliant acting do I have to do before I'm spotted and given lots of money to be a brilliant actor?

Mum was rolling out her cheese pastry when the snake flopped out. She made a strange high-pitched noise like a New York police siren. By the time I reached the kitchen, Dad was picking her up off the floor and she was gasping for air.

'Alfred was in my anchovy toasties!' she whispered. 'I was just going to chop up my pastry when it wriggled.' Now of course I had to pretend I was glad that Alfred had been found.

'So Alfred's still alive,' I cheered. 'Hooray!' I grabbed a saucepan and filled it with lukewarm water from the tap.

'If Mum has a heart attack you're to blame,' hissed my big brother. 'You're such a fool, Alice. If I was your father I'd put you across my knee and beat you with my slipper.'

'If you were my father I'd have a brain the size of an ant's kneecap!' I said, turning off the tap. 'I'm thawing the snake out.' Then I broke open Mum's pastry and popped a rather cold and stiff Alfred into his warm bath.

'Snakes can't swim,' said William.

'Can't they?' I said. Well Alfred couldn't. He'd sunk to the bottom of the pan. I

grabbed him out and rigged up a hammock with a J-cloth and two elastic bands, then stuck him back in the sling so that his body was underwater but his head was out. The colour flooded back into his cheeks.

That was when my big sister reappeared. Apparently, she'd spent a horrible night at her boyfriend's house. He'd made her sleep on the floor in case the beans made her fart.

'What beans?' said mum. 'You didn't eat beans. You hardly eat anything!'

'The beans that *he* made up on the telephone!' shouted Mel, pointing at me. I thought she was going to attack me, but I was wrong. Instead, she lunged forward, grabbed the pan with Alfred in, plonked it on the cooker and turned the heat up full.

'What are you doing?' I squealed.

'Boiled snake,' she said, leaving the room. 'I hate all of you!'

Poor Alfred. In the dustbin, out of the dustbin, in the fridge, out of the fridge, freezing cold one minute, boiling hot the next. It's a wonder he didn't bite anyone. He must be the best-tempered boa constrictor in the world. Either that or the best-cooked.

'First thing in the morning,' growled Dad, 'that snake goes!'

Early bath for me and snake

Me 150 - Them 125

105

Have not slept a wink. Alfred has been making funny gurgling noises all night. When I got up to check on him he was lying perfectly still with his eyes open and a lopsided grin on his face. He looks exactly like Jack Nicholson. I went into Mum and Dad's bedroom and told them Alfred was sick.

'It's three o'clock in the morning,' groaned my dad. 'Go away!'

'But he's ill,' I said. 'I can't chuck him away while he's ill. I might kill him.'

'We'll get rid of him when he's better,' mumbled my mum. 'Go back to bed.'

So now I'm back in bed, but I still can't sleep. Alfred's staring eyes are inside my head. I think he's gone mad. I think he's planning his revenge on me for putting him in the fridge! Why does everything go wrong in my life? How do you tell a snake you're sorry? And why aren't my friends here when I need them?

Friends. That's it! That's what's wrong. Alfred needs friends, a bit of company, someone to talk to. If I buy him some friends he'll like me again and stop wanting to kill me. There is only one problem. Animal friends cost money and I'm broke. I know a man who isn't though.

Unfortunately it was only four thirty in the morning and Dad was still asleep. So I made him a cup of coffee which somehow got spilled *by accident* over his sheets and woke him up. He leapt out of bed like a rocket. 'Dad,' I said, smiling. 'A week ago, I got twenty gold stars . . .'

'Aaaagh! My legs!' he cried. 'Call an ambulance!'

When I got back from

school, Dad was much better. He could walk without screaming. I asked him if he'd give me £30 for getting those gold stars. I was expecting applause. I was expecting whoops of joy and phone calls to relatives telling them how brainy I was. Instead I got this:

'What are gold stars?'

'They're what we get given at school for being good,' I said.

'For being good,' laughed Dad. 'I'm not giving you money for being good, Alistair. You should be good at all times, regardless of money. Goodness is not a shirt you put on in the morning and take off last thing at night. Goodness is something you wear all the time, even in the bath. Like a vest.'

'What happens when the vest is in the wash?' I asked.

'Well you can't wear it then, obviously.'

'So when the vest's in the wash you're bad, are you?'

'Yes,' said Dad, 'definitely. Now fetch us a beer, mate, and I'll give you a fiver.'

I fetched the beer and demanded the fiver, even though Dad called me a 'scrape' and said he hadn't meant it. But the end of the day that was all I had and £5 won't even buy you the back legs of a terrapin. Tomorrow I must earn more before 'Alfred the Mad and Friendless' completely flips his lid and goes on a blood-sucking, poison-pumping, windpipe-wringing rampage.

Mum cooked a special remembrance dinner tonight for the cat Napoleon. There were candles on the table and Dad said a few heartfelt words. Six to be precise.

'Goodbye, Napoleon. You were a cat.' Mel cried and the rest of us looked at the floor.

Vest in wash 150-143

# TUESDAY

My big brother is a pig and I am never giving him a birthday present again, unless I have an infectious disease like chickenpox or mumps then I'll give him that! I went to Mum and asked what jobs she had to earn money and she said, 'None, because I've given them to William.'

'But those were *my* jobs!' I gasped. 'And I've got a mad snake upstairs that needs friends!'

William was washing the car before school and when I went to take the sponge off him, he held me at arm's length and counted out imaginary fifty-pound notes under my nose.

'I hope you drink washing-up liquid by accident and choke to death on soapy bubbles!' I said. 'And while you're doing me favours, give me my Cup Final tickets too. I know you've got them!' But instead of answering, he turned the hose on me and I had to go to school in wet trousers like a Second Year. I have probably got pneumonia now – not that anyone cares.

When I got home, my big brother and sister met me in the hall with big grins. They told me that Mum and Michael had had an argument on the phone. They said that the man in charge of the BBC was furious with *me*, because it was my fault that the recording of Mum's cooking couldn't happen till Friday.

Apparently, according to Mel and William, Mum was on the verge of giving me away to an orphanage! I have written the man at the BBC a letter.

Secret Address,
Atrocity Road,
T—ing

Dear Man at the BBC,
Your wife is safe. Do not try to contact us. If you stop saying I was responsible for Mum's cooking programme not being recorded until Friday, she will be returned unharmed.

Love,
A Terrorist.

PS Don't try to find me, because I won't be there.

Before bed, I made Mum a cup of tea and smiled a lot in her direction.

'Are you happier after that tea?' I asked.

'A bit,' she said.

'Oh good. Would you like one of my sweets?'

'I would,' she said. 'What are they?'

'I've forgotten,' I said. 'But they're not very nice.'

'Well I won't then,' she said. Which was just as well, because I didn't have any. I only offered her a sweet to make her like me, and I only wanted her to like me so that I could ask my next question.

'Mummy, if I promise to be good and stay out of your hair for the next few days can I borrow twenty pounds?'

'Only if you practise your piano,' she said.

I walked into that one!

It was torture, but I did it. Only I didn't have to do it for long, because when I played my third note there was that funny squelching noise again and this time there was another noise, a distant screech like a violin played by a chipmunk or Mr E's hideous howling. But it wasn't Mr E.

112

I opened the lid and discovered a thin and scrawny Napoleon in a corner trying to avoid the hammers as they hit the wires. There was a nasty smell as well. On closer inspection, I discovered to my horror that the piano was full of cat poo, which was why some of the notes had squelched.

with my fingers!

Holding Napoleon at arm's length, I entered the sitting room in triumph, fully expecting a hero's welcome. Instead, what I got was abuse from Mel who accused me

*Brilliant joke, Alistair! I hadn't come downstairs till I'd thought of that one!

___

of deliberately hiding her cat in the piano to upset her.

'If anyone's upset,' I told her, 'it's me. My piano's ruined. The only tune I can play on it now is *Plopsticks*.*'

I mean poor old Mum's set her heart on me having a three-and-a-half-hour lesson this Sunday and now . . .' I turned to Mum with a pained expression on my face,

Move over Brad Pitt, better actor coming through!

'. . . I'm really sorry, Mum, I was sooo looking forward to it . . . but I won't be able to go because I can't practise.'

114

My mum smiled. 'Talking of which,' she said, 'you assured me that you had been practising, Alistair.'

'Oh yes,' I said warily.

'So how come there was a noisy cat inside the piano pooping on your notes and you never noticed?'

'I think I might be deaf,' I said. 'Like Beethoven.'

'I think you might be lying,' she said. 'Like Pinocchio.'

My punishment was to clean out the inside of my piano with a wet J-cloth and a spoon. After Mum had inspected my work she gave me £20.

'You did find the cat after all,' she said generously. 'But from now on it's an hour's piano practise every day and I shall be watching.'

Could come down to penal-
ties, 150-149

I hope Not

115

# WEDNESDAY

Piano practise before school. Dull and Duller. But *after* school, Aaron, Ralph and me took my £25 to the pet shop and bought a few friends for 'Mad Alfie the

Snake' – two geckos, six stick insects and an egg box full of crickets!

The geckos are all right to touch, but the stick insects are yucky and sticky with long spindly legs. I only hope that Alfred doesn't hate them as much as I do or he'll

The crickets smirked like they thought they were specially chosen pets, little knowing that they were in fact gecko food!

never forgive me for rolling him into an
anchovy toastie, and if he doesn't forgive
me I'm dead in my bed!

'What about some live food for Alfred?'
whispered Aaron.

'He'll calm down if he eats.'

'How much are two rats?' I asked the
man.

'A pound a tail,' he said.

'Can it be 60p for those two scrawny
ones?' I asked. The man took every last
penny I had and gave me the two skinny
rats. They had mean, shifty eyes and kept
touching their mouths with their paws.

'See that,' said Ralph. 'They're lab rats.
They're addicted to cigarettes. They need
nicotine. I bet they're alcoholics too. I bet

117

there's nothing they won't do for a drink.'

'Really?' I said. The last thing I needed was two drug-crazed rats nicking money out of Mum's purse to buy cheap cider!

'Got ya!' laughed Ralph. It was his idea of a joke. So I laughed too, but I still didn't like the way those rats were looking at me. The sooner they were Alfred's lunch the happier I'd be.

When I got home, I put the geckos and the stick insects into separate Pyrex casserole dishes and introduced Alfred. 'Geckos and Stick Insects, meet Snake.

Snake, meet Geckos and Stick Insects. You lot can become best mates and play together.' Then I shoved the rats in the cage and introduced them too. 'Snake, Rats. Rats, Snake. Don't get too attached, because he's going to eat you!' At which point Alfred smiled at me and I was forgiven.

Picking up crickets to feed to the geckos is harder than I'd thought. I wasn't going to touch the crickets with my fingers, obviously, so I used Mum's tweezers. Unfortunately I kept tweezing too hard and their legs came off. One of the

← stick insects with legs tweezered off (took me ages to draw these!)

crickets actually popped like an over-stuffed pillow.

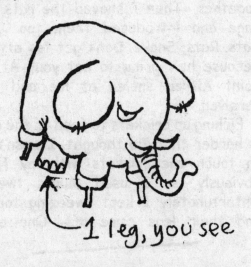

1 leg, you see

More piano practice before bed. *March of The One-Legged Elephant* is the most boring piece of music ever written, employing, as it does, two hundred and sixty three consecutive B flats. Yawn! Yawn! I won't have any trouble sleeping tonight.

My animal army is back to full strength 199-149

# THURSDAY

More piano practice. My poor fingers haven't ached so much since William slammed them in the car door.

On the plus side, Mum has stopped cooking for us! Tomorrow, the kitchen is out of bounds, because they're recording the first programme. Michael is very relieved. It's going out on Sunday and they're way behind schedule. Now we can go back to proper food like fish fingers, pizzas and chips!

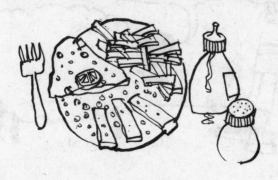

121

I received a reply from
the man at the BBC:

*Dear Mr Terrorist,*
*My wife is perfectly safe thank you. She*
*and I are currently enjoying a lovely break-*
*fast together in our Victorian-style*
*conservatory. The sun is shining and the*
*orange juice is freshly squeezed. In*
*future, I recommend you heed the famous*
*words of Omar Khayam; 'He who pulls the*
*wool over the sheep's eyes must first get*
*to know the sheep.'*
*Yours etc*

I do not understand a word of this letter, but I shall take it as a full apology and quite right too.

After school, Aaron and Ralph came round to check for themselves that Alfred had stopped being a psychopath.

'He's blooming,' said Ralph, 'but your geckos look peaky.'

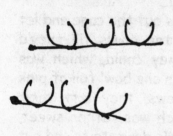

I told him I thought they were hungry.

'And the stickies are shedding their skins,' said Aaron.

It was clear that we had a feeding emergency on our hands. We needed food. Ralph suggested that the Stickies might like a bit of rat.

'Which bit?' I asked. 'The cheek bit, the tail bit or the whiskery bit?'

'The vegetable bit,' said Aaron. 'Stickies are vegetarians.'

'No wonder they're so thin and weedy,' I said. 'Let's raid the kitchen.'

You've never seen so much stuff in one fridge. We took half a dozen bowls each, ran back upstairs and gave the geckos and

123

stickies a slap-up meal. We had no idea what it was, but they seemed to like it. The rats took an interest too. They put their feet on the bars and wiggled their whiskers.

'Go on, give them some,' said Ralph.

'Why?' I said.

'They're on Death Row. Condemned men always get a last meal.'

So we took the rats out the cage and let them run around in the bowls till they'd eaten as much as they could, which was most of everything. In one bowl full of pink mousse and crab claws, they left their little footprints, which was rather sweet. Then we took the bowls downstairs and put them back in the fridge.

After Ralph and Aaron had gone – more piano practice. At this rate I'll have worn out the keyboard by Sunday. I can hear Mrs Muttley's horrible piercing laugh in my head. It is like the whistle of an oncoming train and I am tied to the rails waiting for it to hit me.

It is two o'clock in the morning. The geckos are sleeping on their backs. I have never seen them do this before. The stickies seem OK though, if a little more hyperactive than usual. One stickie has just hurled itself against the glass wall and is lying on its back stunned. It's probably that liver and bacon ice-cream. It has the same effect on me.

One point for crushing the BBC 200-149

The geckos are obviously having a lie-in, because no amount of banging on their Pyrex dish will wake them. I took the lid off and gave them a poke but neither moved. The stickies have calmed down though, despite overnight leg loss. But the best news is that for the first time in a week, Alfred has lifted his head up and is looking at the rats. He must be hungry, because the rats have started winking and waving back at him, and trying to make best friends so he won't eat them.

More piano. Mum says it's a wonderful skill to possess, that one day I'll thank her when I'm earning money playing piano at the Albert Hall. I didn't realize that *March Of the One-Legged Elephant* was so popular with concert-going audiences.

My big brother and sister stopped me at the foot of the stairs. They were both smirking.

'Oh dear, Alice, you're in *such* trouble!' said Mel. 'You might even be sent to live away from home. In an institution with bug-eyed children who wet their beds!' This was the same big sister who'd hung me out of windows when I was four and pointed at police cars. 'They're coming to get you,' she'd said. 'You're going to prison, Alice!' I didn't take any notice of her then and I wasn't taking any notice of her now. But when Napoleon and Mr E suddenly flew out of the kitchen at head height like Superman's cat and dog, I sensed that something was not quite right.

Mum had opened the fridge. Worse than that, Mum had removed the food that she'd spent the last ten days preparing. Worse even than that, Mum had spotted rat-prints in her half-eaten crab mousse.

**'I'M GOING TO HAVE TO START AGAIN!'**

she wailed.

'What's wrong?' I asked innocently. I didn't want her to think I knew anything about the great food robbery.

# 'WHAT'S WRONG?'

she shouted.

## 'What's wrong? I'll tell you what's wrong, Alexander.'

'Alistair,' I whispered, 'but it doesn't matter.'

**'SOMEONE HAS EATEN THE FOOD FOR MY PROGRAMME! I'd prepared everything I needed to "prepare earlier" and now somebody's eaten it!'**

'It wasn't my pets,' I said. 'I don't know who did it. Maybe it was a burglar.'

# 'YES! A RAT BURGLAR!'

she roared, shoving the tiny footprints under my nose.

'It wasn't just the rats,' I said before I could stop myself. 'The geckos and stickies ate stuff too! *By accident*!' Suddenly there was a nasty silence.

Then in a slightly shaky voice my mother whispered, 'Get out of my sight. The programme's going to be cancelled. Everything is ruined!'

That was when Michael appeared with the film crew. They had arrived with a van full of equipment and a lorry full of bacon rolls and biscuits. Mum was sitting on the

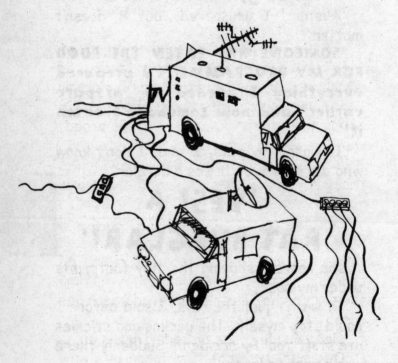

kitchen floor sobbing into a bottle of sherry when William answered the door. 'The patient's in the kitchen,' he said, trying not to smile.

I was in big trouble. I knew that before Michael and Mum staggered out of the kitchen and called us into the hall.

'Children,' she said calmly, 'we will be cooking live!'

'We?' said Mel.

'Because the food has been eaten out of the fridge we cannot record today as planned and I must start again. Tomorrow I will shop and prepare my ingredients. On Sunday, from our kitchen, we will broadcast live to the nation.'

'I still don't get the "we",' said Mel. 'I thought you said it was just *me* who was going to be on telly.'

'If I am to cook live,' said Mum, 'I will need all the help I can get. That means all three of you.' Mel stepped forward to complain, but Mum shut her up by holding the finger-that-must-be-obeyed under her nose.

'Clear Sunday,' she hissed. 'That is all.'

This must be what they mean by every cloud has a silver lining. I do the worst thing I've ever done in my life and my absolutely most awful punishment is to a) get myself back on telly and b) get my

Thank heaven for that

piano lesson cancelled!

*March Of The One-Legged Elephant* is no more. I have burnt the sheet music in the garden and buried the ashes. This is every Christmas, birthday, skive-off-school day rolled into one. I have never ever been this happy! I am totally full of bliss!

At school, when I told the Revengers about my geckos having a long lie-in, Ralph was rather cold and matter-of-fact. 'They're not kipping,' he said. 'They're dead!

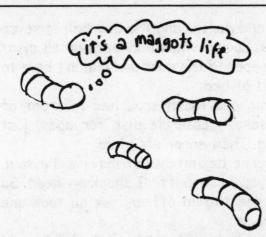

Too much tiramisu!' I said it couldn't be. I was sure I'd seen them move. 'Of course you have,' he said. 'Dead bodies *always* move. It's the maggots!' Aaron asked if he could have a look, because he'd never seen a dead body full of maggots before. I said he could, but he'd have to come early, because I thought tomorrow might be quite a busy day.

Avoided Mum all evening.

A game of two halves - first half 200-250; second half 1493-25011!

# SATURDAY

Ralph and Aaron rang the doorbell at seven o'clock. Luckily Mum had been up all night so she opened the door and I didn't have to get out of bed.

Aaron and Ralph crouched in front of the geckos' casserole dish for ages, just staring. Then Aaron stood up.

'They're definitely not moving,' he said. 'Have you had a sniff?' I shook my head. So Ralph slid the lid off and we all took one step back.

'Now do you believe me?' Ralph said

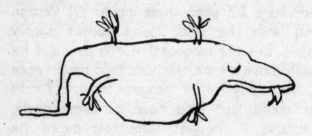

smugly. 'That stink is "dead". "Having a long lie-in" is snoring and stuff.'

'Do you know any hymns?' Aaron asked.

'What for?' I said.

'The funeral.'

'You don't need a funeral for geckos,' Ralph snorted. 'Just feed them to the snake.'

---

But Alfred turned his nose up at dead gecko and looked hopefully at the rats instead. He liked his meat with a bit of chase in it. But now that I'd got to know the rats I turned squeamish.

'Can't do it,' I said. 'I can't feed him rat. All that blood up the walls. It's too cruel.' Alfred would just have to starve.

When Ralph and Aaron had gone, me, Mel and William were lined up in the kitchen.

'I have to go shopping,' said Mum, 'and I need help.'

'Oh no, I've just remembered,' William said suddenly. 'I'm going to the cinema this morning.'

'Me too!' shouted Mel. 'William and I are going to see that new thing with whatsis-name, you know – actor, hair, does a lot of films.'

'And I'm going too!' I said quickly.*

'No you're not,' smirked William, 'It's a fifteen, Alice, so they won't let you in.'

My mother sighed. 'I'll cut you a deal,' she said. 'If you two big ones could go tonight instead, and take Alistair with you . . .'

'Do we have to?' they groaned.

135

'I haven't finished!' snapped Mum. 'I will pay. OK? That means I can have some peace to do my cooking.'

'But what about the shopping?' sulked my big brother. 'I'll be too tired to go to the cinema if I've been shopping too.'

'Me too,' whined my big sister. 'And I won't have time to phone my Lukey.'

'Fine!' said my mum sharply. 'Alistair can come shopping with me now, just so long as you two promise to take him off my hands this evening.' *Take him off my hands!* What was I now? A wart?

Shopping was a nightmare. Shopping is *always* a nightmare, because everyone always knows Mum. 'Hello, Celia. What's cooking?' If I had ten pounds for every time I'd heard that, I could buy all the geckos in the world. Inside the super-market people asked Mum's advice on recipes, or told Mum how their shepherd's pie was nicer than hers, or took things out of our shopping trolley and walked off with them, saying stupid things like, 'Well if it's good enough for Celia Fury it's good enough for me!' For three and a half hours it was nothing but *aisle-aisle-aisle, food-food-food, bored-bored-bored!* But when Mum

my very own cut out and keep 'smile when you're shopping' mask

looked round I made sure it was *smile-smile-smile*, and *happy to be here-happy to be here-happy to be here*, because I didn't want to mess up my big TV break. When we finally got to the checkout some mad,

bearded lady ruffled my hair and said to Mum, 'Ooh, isn't he sweet, Celia! He is yours I take it?'

I stood on tiptoe and whispered in her ear, 'No I'm not. My parents were poisoned to death by one of her prawn recipes and she's had to look after me ever since.' The old lady dropped her eggs and went as pink as the prawns in her basket.

Later that evening, I was 'taken off Mum's hands' by William and Mel and Luke the Puke. From the way Mel had drooled over Luke I was expecting a cross between Brad Pitt and Tom Cruise. In actual fact, with his matted hair and long swinging arms, he looked like an orang-utan and Mel was all over him like a flea.

When we walked down the road towards the cinema they held hands, so I did fart

REALLY EMBARRASSING!

noises behind Mel's bottom and he laughed, which made Mel really cross.

'Grow up!' she squeaked. 'Act your age!'

'I am acting my age,' I said. 'I'm eleven. Farts are funny.'

But in the cinema I should have acted older. The film was a '12' and the man in the booth said I was only eight.

'Pants!' I said. 'What are we going to do now that we can't go to the cinema?'

'Wrong!' laughed William. '*You* can't go to the cinema, but *we* can.' Traitors! Hanging was too good for them.

'Don't run out and play with the cars,' said Mel. 'Wait here till we come out.'

'But that won't be for three hours,' I said.

'That's the price you pay for being little!' said William. 'Sit!'

'Don't I even get any chocolate raisins?'

'SIT!' So I sat outside on the cold stone step while they went inside the warm, comfortable, luxury cinema to watch the film.

In the next ten minutes I felt hate, loathing and revenge. Then I nipped round to the fire exit and waited for someone to come out. I slipped inside and found my way into the auditorium. It was dark and the film was loud so nobody knew I was there. I fell to the floor, commando style, and crawled up the aisle on my belly. I could see my big brother with his feet up on the seat in front and my big sister sitting next to him. The boyfriend was at the far end pretending to watch the film, but really taking sneaky looks down Mel's T-shirt.

I crawled between the seats and stopped behind my big brother, then 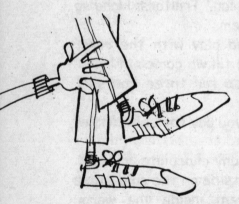 pushed my arm through the gap and stroked his leg. William leapt up with a huge shiver and 'Aagh!' but couldn't see who'd done it.

'What are you doing?' hissed Mel.

'Did you just stroke my leg?' he asked.

'Don't be gross,' she said.

'Sit down!' came a shout from behind. So William sat down.

I gave it three minutes then stuck my hand through another gap and stroked the

TTHWWACK!

boyfriend's leg! Drippy boyfriend only thought it was big sister, didn't he! He stroked her leg back and she slapped him. Whack! Bullseye! He was stunned. He didn't know what had hit him. Mel Ha ha!

Meanwhile Mel was sitting there all offended so I crept up behind and slapped *her*. It worked a treat. She thought it was the boyfriend slapping her back and slapped him *again*. Only this time she chucked her Coke and popcorn over him as well. Then she left. It was brilliant. It was like everything I'd planned in my head just happened the way it was meant to.

It was just a shame that William had to see me.

When we got home I had two dead legs and Chinese burns on both my wrists. I tried to explain that it was only a joke, but Mel was in hysterics, because Luke had

dumped her, and William had really been enjoying the film when the manager had thrown us out. So basically I had ruined both their lives. Then while Mel bawled in her room, William put my head down the loo. 'You owe me five pounds,' he said.

'What for?' I bubbled.

'For the wasted ticket, Alice.'

'Then you owe me five pounds too,' I said.

'No, I do not.'

'Yes you do!' I shouted, pushing him off

and standing up. 'For all the pain and hard-ship you've ever caused me. For all the loneliness. For all the times I've tried to be your friend and you wouldn't listen. For leaving me outside the cinema. For stealing my Cup Final tickets. For calling me "little" and that stupid name, "Alice". In short, William Fury, you big pig, you owe me five pounds for being your little brother!' That shut him up.

During supper everyone was quiet. Mum was thinking about recipes, Dad was thinking about the round of golf he couldn't play tomorrow, Mel was crying over lost love and William was watching me.

Afterwards, when we were upstairs, he said, 'You won't ever say what you said to me earlier in front of Mum and Dad, will you?' He was worried I might shop him.

'That depends,' I said. It was fun having all the power! 'That depends on whether you tell me if Cocoa Pops called or not.'

William nodded his head. 'They did,' he said. 'You only came third though, so you've only won one ticket. They said you should pick it up tomorrow from the Wembley box office.'

'Are you serious?' I grinned.

He nodded again. It's a sunny day in Heaven! I knew I'd won. I knew it!

I am the greatest! Me 2,356,223-Them 251

# SUNDAY

Up early, because the telly people are coming at eight o'clock to set up for tonight's live broadcast. I'm quite nervous, but I bet all the great TV superstars go through the same thing – Les Dennis, Richard Madeley, Keith Chegwin and Orville. It's a humbling thought that when I appear on TV in front of millions I shall be more famous than the Queen!

Michael kept us out of the kitchen all day while Mum rehearsed for the cameras. Dad sat in the living room feeling left out, Mel spent all day in her bedroom doing her make-up, and William and I played Paper, Rock, Scissors and pretended to get on.

At four o'clock we were allowed into the kitchen. We were all excited and Mum was smiling – that fixed smile she does when she's not enjoying birthday parties but pretends that she is.

I won even though he says he let me.

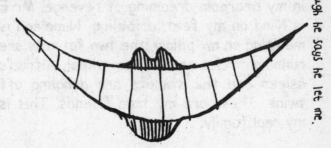

'Right,' she said. 'You know I said you'd all be helping me today . . .' This was the bit I'd been waiting for! 'Well I'm sorry, Alistair, but you're too little.' At first I didn't hear what she said. I mean I heard it, but it didn't seem real. Then it struck home.

'Too little!' I gasped. 'Too little! Why is "little" always so bad? And how can I be too little for telly? Get a smaller camera.'

'It's my fault,' said Michael. 'But the show's live, Alistair, and I can't take the risk that you might mess things up. Mel and William are only handing plates to your mother. They'll hardly be seen at all.' Too little! I was choked. It's not my fault I've got the family's midget gene!

It is 4.30. The show goes on air at 6.30. Everyone except me is downstairs doing a dress rehearsal without food. I am sitting in my bedroom dreaming of revenge. Mr E is lying on my feet, dribbling, Napoleon is moulting on my pillow, the two fat rats are running circles round their wheel, Alfred's asleep and the stickies are dangling off twigs. These are my true friends. This is my real family.

5.45 – I've just had a flash.
I phoned up Aaron.

'Peanut butter and jam sandwiches,' I whispered.

'Peanut butter and jam sandwiches.' That was Aaron. 'Speak, fellow Revenger.'

'I need to get my mum back for something horrible she's just done, fellow Revenger.'

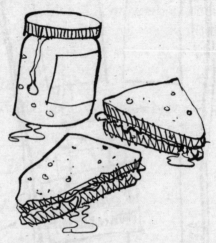

'Hang on, I'll get the other fellow Revenger on the phone too.'

'Is Ralph there?' I asked.

'Ssh!' hissed Aaron. 'No names!'

'Sorry,' I said.

'Peanut butter and jam sandwiches,' said Ralph coming to the phone.

'Peanut butter and jam sandwiches,' I

replied.

'How can I help you, fellow Revenger?' That was Ralph again.

'Like I told Aaron,' I said. 'I've got to get back at my mum big time.'

'That's easy,' said Ralph. 'Strike at the heart!'

'I don't understand,' I said.

'Put these six words in the right order,' said Ralph, 'and you will have your answer. *Programme, cookery, live, the, up* and *mess.*'

'Oh,' I said slyly, cracking the secret code. 'Yes of course!'

6.30 – When Michael called for 'absolute quiet!' and counted down from ten to zero, I crept downstairs with two boxes hidden under my jumper. If I stood on the third step and looked through the glass window above the kitchen door I could see Mum talking to the camera and taking plates of food from my big brother and sister. Mel

was smiling so hard her face was in danger of splitting, and William was trying to look cool by *not* smiling and doing everything dead casual. I could see Dad in the sitting room watching the programme go out live on the telly. He was snoring. Nobody was watching me though, which was just what I wanted.

I crept out the front door, climbed over the back gate and released my weapons through the cat flap. One snake, two rats and six limping stick insects! Then I pressed my nose against

the kitchen window and waited for the fun
to begin!

heads explode

glass shatters

Eight million people heard Mel scream
when a rat ran up her tights. It was being
chased by Napoleon, who'd heard the
pitter-patter of tiny rodent feet and had
crashed through the cat flap to catch
them. Mel fell backwards and knocked her
head against a shelf of pots and pans and
brought the whole lot crashing to the
floor. Michael clamped his hand over her
mouth to try and stop her screaming, but a
stickie dropped off the ceiling into his

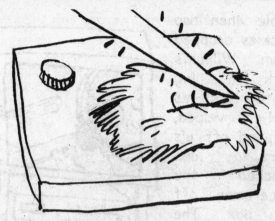

hair, which started him screaming as well. He snatched off his wig and chucked it away, but it landed right in front of Mum, and the stickie fell on the chopping board, where she was showing the nation how to prepare okra. Then while Mel was dragged out and Michael got a good slapping to shut him up, Alfred made his first appearance behind Mum's head. He was hungry now and wanted some rat. He slid over her shoulder and set off after his lunch, knocking all Mum's food off the work surface. He was a good hunter though. He got the rats cornered next to the bread bin, right in front of the camera. Then he wrapped his tail around both rats together, dislocated his jaw and was just about to eat them

whole when two stickies dropped down William's neck. Big brother lost his cool, yelped, whipped off his shirt, and knocked the cameraman off his box. The camera went up in the air and took shots of

the ceiling, while Mum kept on talking as if nothing was wrong. But it was, because when the camera was turned the right way up again, Mum had to show the viewers all her lovely ingredients with her hair crawling with stickies! And behind her Mr E had grabbed Michael's wig in his jaws and was shaking it to death like a rabbit. And behind Mr E, Napoleon and Alfred were locked in a tug of war over the rats, until Alfred's tail lost its grip, the rats tumbled free, Napoleon fell off the counter and the rats, much to every viewer's surprise, ate Alfred. It was quite a rare TV event so I'm told. Nobody had ever seen food eat the eater before, and Napoleon decided not to tangle with the rats after all.

That was when I felt a hand on my collar.

'There you are!' said Michael. 'We've got a problem.'

'I didn't do it!' I said. 'It was an accident. It wasn't me.'

'What are you talking about?' he said. 'I need your help.'

'I thought I was too little,' I said bitterly.

'Not any more,' he said. 'Your brother and sister are too scared to go back into the kitchen while those rats and stick things are in there, and they're meant to be tasting the food at the end of the programme. I need you to do it, Alistair, I need you to walk into that kitchen and save the day!'

'But I hate my mum's food,' I said. 'It

makes me sick. I can't pretend to like it.'

'I'm afraid you have to,' said Michael. 'It's called acting.'

But my stomach was starting to feel queasy. 'So what's she cooking?'

'Tooting green curry with lemongrass rice, extra large chilli-balls and a side dish of okra in live yoghurt.'

'What's okra?' I said suspiciously.

KEEP OUT! ⚠ BIOWOTSIT HAZARD

'It's green,' said Michael, 'and looks like fingers, but it's covered in yoghurt so you won't see a thing.'

'And if I do this I get to be a television celebrity?'

'Definitely,' he said.

'Then I'll do it,' I said.

I couldn't stop grinning. I grinned at

Michael. I grinned at Mel. I grinned at William. I even grinned at Mum while she talked to the country with a rat on her

shoulder. For the first time in my life I was BIGGER than my brother and sister. I was the chosen one!

I was told to wait behind the camera while Mum finished her cooking. The kitchen looked like a hurricane had just blown through it. There was food and yoghurt and bits of tomato everywhere. Then suddenly everyone was looking at me and Michael pushed me on.

'This is Alexander,' said my mum, 'my littlest.'

'Alistair,' I hissed. How could she get my name wrong with the whole world watching?

'He's going to help me taste what I've cooked. Come and sit beside me,' she said, patting the chair next to her. The camera followed me to the table and stuck its nose in the food I was about to eat. The curry was green, the lemongrass rice had sticks of bamboo in it, and the okra looked like fat twigs in white custard. A plate with everything on was plonked in front of me and I was told to tuck in. I held my breath, put on a smile and started to eat. Surprisingly I didn't mind the taste, although the okras were a bit woody. In fact everything went rather well until, after several forkfuls, something twitched on my plate. It was one of the okras. It swam through the custard, stood up, lurched forward and hopped across the chilliballs! And just as it did so, my lips were prised open and a thin, sticky leg popped out!

My stomach turned over. My mouth filled with

158

vmmph

water. I had to remember that I was live on air. I had to remain calm. I had to behave like a TV superstar, but I couldn't! I spat out what was in my mouth and sprayed the camera with yoghurt. Then I looked down at my plate and saw to my horror that what I'd been eating wasn't okra at all. It was a stick insect! My evil mother had cooked my pets! I was a cannibal!

I'm not sticking around there

'I can't keep it down!' I screamed. But my cruel mother ignored my cries and kept smiling.

'And that's all we've got time for,' she said to the nation.

'Here it comes!' My face turned green and I clamped my hand over my mouth.

'Join me again same time next week.'

'MUMMY!'

159

I'm fed up with this scoring rubbish. It's stupid! I'm not doing it anymore.

---

'So happy cooking and good . . .' She didn't make it to 'bye', because that was when my mouth erupted in a fountain of pink, orange and green, and eight million people saw what I'd had for breakfast.

Another early night.
Can't sleep a wink – I can still feel that leg wiggling!

# MONDAY

Three men in white coats took Mum off to hospital last night so Dad's taken the week off work to look after us. I think I might be back in Coventry, but nobody will tell me so I don't know for sure.

After school, I took a bus to Wembley Stadium to collect my FA Cup Final ticket, but when I got there nobody knew anything about it – except my big brother of course, who thinks it's the best joke in the world to send me all the way across London to pick up *nothing*! This is war! I have called an  emergency meeting of the Revengers to discuss a plan of action. This time my revenge will be total!

Dad's just called supper, so I'd better go. I shall, however, check that Mr E and Napoleon are safe before I eat a morsel. I shall never get over the shame of belonging to a family that eats its own pets.

Hello, Alice. Big brother and big sister here.
You're still downstairs eating supper. Guess
what we've just found under your bed. My-
oh-my, what a lot of words! Now then,
naughty little brother, how shall we make
you pay?

Love

M & W

P.S. Remind us - it's Pamela Whitby you love,
isn't it?

For Max and Harry
who can show this to their friends

# My Daily Diary

*This diary belongs to* Alistair Fury

*Age* 11

*Address* 47 Atrocity Road, Tooting, England

*Country of Birth* Slaveland *Nationality* Slavish

*Place of Birth* That's disgusting! Where does everyone get born from?

*Next of kin* I have kin that are 'next' in the sense that I clear their hairs out of the sink before I can brush my teeth and they're next in line for the payback treatment, but 'next' in the sense of the people who love me most in the world no matter what . . . I have none. I am as an orphan.

*Any distinguishing scars* Only mental and they're too deep to see. Except they may show through in my writing, because I'm only human after all. As it says in Shakespeare's Two Merchants of Verona by somebody whose name I forget — 'If you stab me with a compass and twiddle the sharp bit round in the hole, do I not bleed?'

*Profession* Hit boy

*Hobbies* Revenge

# Notes

'Bring out your dead! Bring out your dead! Come on everyone sling 'em out the

windows!' This is an authentic and true reconstruction of what it must have been like during the plague. Around our house, it is like that again only without the dead bodies, the shouting and the plague. We've got the flu. I have been ill with this fatal lurgy for nearly five days and have missed school all this week. So in case I should die here is my last will and testicle.

# The Last Will and Testicle of Alistair Fury

## To the Revengers

I leave all my evil thoughts, plus my armoured go-kart-building diagrams and my plans for breaking into the zoo and releasing all the tigers through the sewers so they can pop up in Miss Bird's class at school and eat her, obviously. I also leave them my brain (which may *not* go to medical science, however much mad scientists might want to harness its genius) so that any brilliant thoughts I might have in the future can belong to my best friends too.

## To my family

I leave my toenails, because they will keep growing for ever, and one day will be so big that they will fill the house in every room and therefore I will have got a great revenge on my big brother and sister and my uncaring parents by making them move out and become homeless.

I am of sound mind.

Alistair Fury

Alistair Fury

# THURSDAY

My first mistake was getting ill; my second was getting better, because now I am a slave. The rest of my family has caught flu too and is blaming me for giving it to them. Mum and Dad can't work and my big brother and sister, William and Mel, can't go to school. Nor apparently can they get out of bed, make a cup of tea, switch on the radio, scratch their noses or warm the loo seat for themselves! I think I must have got into a time machine and travelled back to Victorian England, because I am nothing more than a scullery maid!

Which is brilliant, because that means my TV-chef mum can't cook, so we can't be poisoned!

It is outrageous. When I complain about my slave duties, I am told to shut up, because it is my fault that everyone's in bed in the first place and I must suffer too. ➝

Which I will do silently, but only so I have a reason to take revenge on my family later!

'So stop being so inconsiderate,' said William. 'If you hadn't got us all so terribly

ill, Alice, we'd all be being nice to
you.'

He could start by *not* calling me
Alice. I AM A BOY! I have conkers
in my pocket to prove it.

What's with this 'we're *all* so
terribly ill' rubbish? Mum is ill. I
can tell that by the way she keeps trying to
get up and do stuff, but faints every time
she does.

And Dad is ill, because he hasn't been to
work at the leisure centre (where as the
manager he earns more than a Second
Division footballer) for a week. Actually

Dad is more than ill, he's dying! At least that's what he says, and he should know because he reads *Gray's Anatomy* and *The Complete Home Medical Encyclopaedia* all the time.

But William and Mel are having a laugh. Over the last twenty-four hours these are just some of the things I've had to do for my big brother and sister.

'Alistair! Run me a bath. Not too hot and not too cold. And Alistair, don't leave the house in case I need you to pass me a moistened cotton bud to de-wax my ears.'

'Alistair! The radio needs new batteries.'

'Alistair! Change my sheets.'

'Alistair! I need another magazine from the newsagent.'

'Alistair! The video's finished.'

'Alistair! I can't reach my tissues.'

'Alistair!'

'What?'

'Did you put sugar in my tea?'

'Yes.'

'Then it needs more stirring. Would you do it for me?'

Never a please or thank you. Just 'Alistair!' then orders.

And Mel's only staying in bed so she can

be well and beautiful again for next weekend when her new boyfriend, Andy, is taking her out for dinner at the Ritz. At least that's what Mel's expecting.

She said to me. 'My new boyfriend's rich. He's got a car.'

'What sort?' I said.

'A Ford Anglia I think.'

'Ooh,' I said. 'Classy.'

'It is, isn't it?' she said.

'Oh yes, it's like a Porsche,' I said.

'A Porsche!' she squealed. 'I knew he was rich!'

'So where's he taking you on this date?' I asked.

'I don't know,' she said. 'It's a secret. Probably the Ritz!'

'Only probably?' I said. 'No way. It's a dead cert!'

Anyway the point is, how ill can Mel be if she can spend two hours a night giggling on the phone to Mr Hot Rod?

I'm exhausted. Home is like a hospital and it is making me ill.

Ha ha! If she believes this she must be iller than I thought - ill in the head!

171

# FRIDAY

Feel strong enough to go back to school this morning, but I know that Miss Bird, my scummy form teacher, will only shout at me for being away. Miss Bird is like that. She bears grudges. Me, Aaron and Ralph call her Pigeon because she walks like she's got Nelson's Column stuck up her bottom – all little mincey steps and a great big pecking hooter. Her nose is bigger than a giant eagle's and that's the truth. She also has a temper like a spitting volcano,

MISS BIRD

172

which means that unless you like being covered in flecks of red-hot gob it's best to either stay on her good side or buy yourself a pair of facial windscreen wipers.

Last time I saw her she thrust my English exercise book under my nose. 'Your handwriting is a scrawl,' she said. 'It looks like an army of blind ants meandering pointlessly across the page. It looks – and

I hope any worms listening will forgive this slur – like a drunken worm with diarrhoea!' To prove her point she then read out a sentence from my last essay in front of the whole class. '*Tar pig war fuss of sandal. In pickled inner up of the cow pit and skunk off in toe the slalom, digging its tall Belinda tit.*'

'That wasn't what I wrote,' I said.

'Oh really?' she replied, with uncalled-for sarcasm.

'Perhaps you'd care to read what you did write then.'

I had a go, but even I found it tricky. *'The dog was full of shame. It picked itself up off the carpet and slunk off into the shadows, dragging its tail behind it.'*

She crossed her arms with a satisfied grunt and called me stupid.

So when Mel and William told me to stay off school for the sake of my health I didn't take much persuading. But at 9.01 a.m., once school registration was done, they stopped being nice to me and treated me like a slave again.

'If you don't answer to our every whim,' said Will, 'we'll tell Miss Bird that you skived off today when you were perfectly healthy.'

'And in future, if you want to quit your job as our nurse,' said Mel, 'you've got to give us at least three months' notice.' If this is a job *why* am I not getting *paid*?

'Because we're family,' said Dad. 'You look after us because you love us. You'd feel awful if you went off to school and never saw me alive again!'

'No I wouldn't,' I said. 'There'd be one less person to cook supper for.' Which

174

He thinks nobody knows about the empty bottles, but when he turns over in his sleep it sounds like he's got a milk float in bed with him.

---

made Dad cry. It was a joke! Honestly, sometimes Dad is such an over-emotional girl! Maybe aspirins, nose sprays and secret bottles of beer under the mattress do that to a man!

I have a way with food that makes me think that when I grow up I will be Jamie Oliver.

Cooked lunch for all – frozen peas and rice pudding.

In the middle of cooking, Mum fell into the kitchen. If Mum's fans could have seen her with her scarlet face, her hair sticking up like a toothbrush, and her eyes all puffy like a rolled-up pair of rugby socks, they'd never have watched her TV cookery show again. Tried sending her back to bed, but she was away with the fever fairies.

Drama Queen

'I'm a mother,' she cried. 'My children need feeding! Soup! That's what we need. Soup!'

Then Will joined in, shouting downstairs from his bedroom. 'Calling Nurse Alice! Report to your brother's bedside immediately. The pages of my book need turning.'

apples

Mum passed out on the floor with a ham bone and a stick of celery in her hands. Martyrs like Mum are hard work, but skivers like Will and Mel are evil!

Mrs Muttley, my big-boned piano teacher, just called. Don't know why she bothers to use the phone. Her screechy voice is so loud I can hear her without it. She wanted to know why I had missed my piano lesson yesterday. I told her I was ill. She said, 'You're never too ill to play piano.'

I said, 'Yesterday, my fingers were chopped off in a lawnmower accident.'

Blessed silence. I heard her gulp. How am I going to explain the magical re-growth of my fingers when I see her next Thursday?

I need a holiday.

# SATURDAY

Full English breakfast in bed ordered by everyone, because it is the weekend. What is a full English breakfast? Found croissant in the freezer and some Bavarian cheese. Sounds pretty English to me. Faces full of disappointment when I delivered it.

Phoned Ralph on his new mobile.

'Peanut butter and jam sandwiches,' I said. This was our secret club's pass-phrase to let the other person know they were talking to another Revenger.

Ralph's voice changed immediately. He put on a French accent. 'Speak fellow Revenger,' he said. 'I have peeled back the ears.'

I told him I didn't want to be a home-nurse anymore. 'Easy,' he said. 'The best way to stop someone being ill is to give them nasty medicine.'

'But I haven't got any nasty medicine,' I said. 'And I can't exactly go to a doctor and ask for nasty medicine if all I want it for is revenge.'

'Of course you can,' said Ralph. 'It just depends if he's a real doctor or not!'

Ralph and Aaron came round and helped me work out a cunningly simple plan to pay back my evil brother and sister. I will take

their pictures with a Polaroid camera, then I will tell them that because they are too ill to move I will show the pictures to a doctor for his diagnosis. I'm not going to

really. All I'm going to do is write out a pretend prescription and pass it off as the doctor's, which isn't going to be hard, because every doctor in the world has unreadable handwriting, just like I do! Then I'll pretend to go to a chemist to get the prescription, but instead I'll actually mix up a nasty medicine in the kitchen. And after one huge dose each they won't want another so they'll get better instantly and I'll be released from their slave-master grip!

Phew!

When I took Mel's photo she was sitting up in bed with lumps of pink tissue paper hanging damply from her left nostril. 'I look awful,' she said.

'That's the idea,' I told her. 'So the doctor can see what you really look like.'

'You won't ever show these photos to

anyone else, will you?' she said.

'Never,' I said, thinking, *What a brilliant idea!*

Will was half-asleep with his bum crack showing and a bubble of snot on his tongue. Perfect!

When Dad heard what I was doing, he asked to have *his* photo taken too. 'I want the doctor to see me as well,' he said.

But I wasn't giving nasty medicine to Dad. He could stop my pocket money. 'No. You're too far gone, Dad,' I said. 'You've said yourself that you're going to die, so it's a waste of a film, isn't it? And it's not cheap this Polaroid stuff. About £120 for three photos I think.' Anything to do with spending money usually shuts Dad up. He cried again.

Spent the night forging.

8.00 a.m. – Produced the handwritten prescription and showed it to Mel and William so that they'd think it was real.

'But doctors aren't open on Sunday mornings,' said Will suspiciously. 'So how did you get it?'

'This one is,' I said, thinking as fast as I could. 'He's started a Sunday surgery for people who hurt their knees and get clapping blisters in church.' Not my best lie ever.

'I'll just go and pick it up at the chemist,' I said quickly, running out before they saw me blush.

Pretended to go to the chemist.

All I did really was walk round the block four times till I thought I'd been away long enough. Actually, I *had* to stop walking. I was getting funny looks from a huge man in a balaclava who had locked himself out of his car and was trying to get back in with a metal coat-hanger. He called me a 'nosy little beggar' and threatened to punch me in the bracket if I walked past again. So I didn't.

When I got back I sneaked into the kitchen and made their pretend medicine in the blender, using olive oil, pepper sauce, a whole turnip, anchovy paste, worms and lemon washing-up liquid. It was all going brilliantly, until Mum suddenly lurched into the kitchen to make soup for lunch. I tried to hide my potion by casually lying across the blender, but she asked what I was doing.

'Oh, I'm making soup too,' I said stupidly, to get her off my case.

'What an angel,' she said. 'Bring it up when it's ready.'

What could I do? I'm not a soup chef! I don't know how to make real soup like Mum does. She boils up bones and stuff and

---

makes it the same way as cavemen did hundreds of years ago. She keeps a box of bones in the garden shed. When she wrote her last book *Smells From a Soup Kitchen*, she bought from the butcher every bone that's ever been stripped out of every animal that's ever lived, so she could make soup all day.*

I couldn't even make soup out of a tin, because we don't have any. As a TV chef Mum disapproves of tins. And I only had 7p on me and soup costs more. So what was I to do?

'Alistair!' That was Mum calling again. 'Ready for your soup now!' Mixed up some tomato ketchup with cold water and passed it off as *gestapo*, that cold Spanish soup. Then after everyone had left it and I had cleared up their trays, I gave Mel and William their revenge medicine!

Actually after all that, it was a rubbish payback, because I was up all night with them being sick into buckets. And when I tried to wash the sick down the bath, little lumps

184

kept sticking in the plughole. I had to use Mum's mascara brush to poke them through.

In between mop-ups, I had a dream. A nightmare really, about my handwriting, in which everything was highly significant.

# my highly significant nightmare dream

*I am in a supermarket, shopping for my sick family. Me and the lovely Pamela Whitby are shopping together off one long shopping list, like a husband and wife. She is wearing a cardigan and slippers and looks happy, but this can't last, because we're working off a list that's been handwritten by me and neither of us can read it. So I ask a fellow shopper if he can. The man draws a gun and grabs me.*

*'If I read it right,' he screams, 'this note says you're the only son of an oil billionaire.'*

The loveliest girl in the class, but don't tell anyone

185

'No. It says I need cheese,' I said. 'And loo paper.'

'I am taking you hostage. Nobody try to stop me!'

And I'm kidnapped. My mouth is gagged and I can't speak, so as I'm dragged down the pavement I hand out notes to passers-by which say Help! and Get the Police! but they can't read my writing, so nobody helps. And suddenly I find myself dumped on a desert island by this kidnapper and told that I'll be staying there till the ransom's paid, but I know it never will be. So I chuck bottles into the sea with notes inside begging to be rescued, and the bottles wash up on a beach full of happy tourists, which, as it turns out, is only about fifty yards away across the bay. But of course nobody can read what I've written on my notes. So the happy tourists go on wearing silly hats and rubbing each other's fat red bodies with cooking oil, while I'm stuck on this island for ever.

Weird or what?

# MONDAY

Woke up to find my big brother and sister glaring at me in a hurtful manner, because I am going to school and not staying at home to look after them like Indian princes.

'I have to go to school,' I told them. 'If I don't, Pigeon'll give me Saturday morning detentions till the end of my school life!'

'Peanut butter and jam sandwiches,' said Mel, with a cunning smile.

'What do you mean?' I gasped.

'We know what you tried to do to us last night,' she said. 'When I was sick I tasted lemon washing-up liquid.'

That made me feel awful, not to say a little scared that they might tell Mum and Dad I'd tried to poison them, so I made them both tea and toast in bed and ironed William's pyjamas. And that made me late for school.

The class was silent when I walked in.

187

Miss Bird fixed me with her beady eyes, like a psychopathic magpie. 'So good of you to join us, Fury. Would it be more convenient if every morning we simply started school twenty minutes later to let you wake up?'

I thought she was being serious. 'Is that possible?' I asked, to which the answer was a low-flying textbook that scraped past my ear. And that was the high spot of the lesson.

very close

Anxious to get a message to Aaron and Ralph I wrote a note on a scrap of paper and passed it along the line. It read: Meet break. Same place only different. Eat this note when you have read it.

Unfortunately Aaron was caught with his

mouth full. Pigeon picked the soggy paper off his back teeth, carefully unfolded it and read it aloud. I could see from her ears going red that something was wrong.

'*Miss Bird has a huge beaky nose like a pigeon! Don't let the nasty witch read this,*' she hissed.

'No!' I shouted. 'That's my bad hand-writing again. I didn't write that!' But she didn't want to know what I'd written and I got that detention. After school tomorrow.

Us Revengers can no longer use the Second Year loos for our meetings. The Headmistress banned us after Second Year mothers complained about the extra washing their children kept bringing home during last term's unexplained Damp Trouser Epidemic. So we used the *First* Year loos for our break time meeting and as usual Ralph stood guard at the door so that no First Years could get in.

I showed my fellow Revengers the photos of Mel and William. We all agreed that my big brother and sister looked so repulsive that these photos would be brilliant weapons for the future.

Then I brought up the problem with the pass-phrase. 'William and Mel have cracked it,' I said. 'Mel winked when she said "peanut butter and jam sandwiches" to me this morning.' Aaron gasped.

'That's a security beach,' he said.

'Is that like a beach where everyone's got a bodyguard?' asked Ralph.

'Something like that,' I said. 'Look, if we were MI5 we'd all have to commit suicide now to protect our secret identities.'

'Would we?' gulped Ralph.

'Yeah, by swallowing exploding pens or sharing a shower with a scorpion, that sort of thing.'

CANAL No 5

Do i really smell that bad?

190

There was only one thing to do. 'Well, I won't do it,' said Ralph. 'I won't kill myself!'

'No. Invent a new code word,' I said. Everyone agreed it was a shame, because *peanut butter and jam sandwiches* was a good one, but we had to do what we had to do, which we did.

Aaron went first. 'How about peanut butter and *jelly* sandwiches?'

'Don't you think we should move away from the peanut butter theme?' said Ralph.

'Keep the jam you mean?'

'Well maybe get rid of the jam, too,' Ralph said. 'Do without any reference to stuff that's spread on toast.'

'OK. How about *marmalade cats like cream*.' That was Aaron again.

'That's fine,' said Ralph, 'but it's still got a jar of spread in it.'

'I know, but that's the clever bit. That's what'll fool 'em, because you can't spread a marmalade cat.'

'Well you can,' I

said, 'but you've got to run it over with a car first.' *Marmalade cats like cream* it was.

Finally we discussed the problem of Aaron's birthday treat on Saturday. His mum said he could take three friends out for a film and a burger chaser. There was me and Ralph and one free space.

'I've invited Pamela Whitby,' he said.

My heart skipped a beat. I have long admired Pamela Whitby. Just the sight of her brings me up in a pash-rash. 'So what's the problem?' I asked brightly.

'You,' he said. 'You've got to come. I'm not asking Pamela if you duck out at the last minute because of nursing duties.'

'I'm coming,' I said. 'No question.' Then. 'By the way did she say anything when she heard I was going to be there?'

'She said "Alistair Who?" And when I told her who, she said to tell you that she doesn't love you, because she still can't remember who you are or what your face looks like, but she doesn't hate you either. Although she said she was sure she *would* if you're anything like every other boy she's ever met.'

I was in heaven. Pamela Whitby had

My Great-Uncle Crawford (Granny Constance's older brother) told me about love once. He said, 'If you can't kiss a girl without standing on a box, find another girl.' Great-Uncle Crawford and me are the same height, so we see things from the same perspective. He's 104 years old, a tiny, shrunken man, who's lived in Ireland all his life. He's so small we call him the leprechaun, and sometimes he can stand at a bar for hours waiting for a drink and the barman doesn't know he's there!

We left the First Year loos with howls of First Year dampness wringing in our ears.

Got home to mega mess. Mum had obviously been trying to make soup again. There were bones everywhere. I'm sure out neighbours think we're cannibals, because of the constant smell of boiled bones. I put them back in the garden shed. Then noticed the new shiny copper hood over the hob that had just been fitted to extract Mum's evil cooking smells. The workmen who installed it had dumped a huge pile of bricks and dust on the floor, which had obviously been left for me to clear up. What I need is a witch doctor to wave his magic wand and make my skiving family well again, or better still, a terrifying witch to scare them all out of bed! *Eureka!*

Have just looked up *witch* in Yellow Pages. It said *See under Covens*, but there was nothing there either. Except for one advert:

# Bill Nash

## Electrical Engineer.

## All kitchen appliances repaired.

I think Bill Nash has been misfiled.

Had a brilliant idea at school. Aaron said, 'Haven't you got a granny who's a monster? The one who shaves and carries an electric cattle prod in her handbag in case a refugee asks her for money?'

'Granny Constance!' I said.

'That's her,' said Aaron. 'She's a sort of witch. Why don't you go round and ask her tonight?'

'Don't be stupid,' I said. 'How will I get out of the house without William and Mel suspecting something's up?'

'Take Mr E for a walk,' he said.

'What!' I said. 'Take Mr E for a walk! What planet are you from, Aaron? Nobody takes Mr E for a walk! He's a pug dog with a hideous beige-coloured face that looks like someone's kicked it flat with a boot. He's so disgustingly ugly it's embarrassing to be seen on the streets with him!'

196

I think they'd be doing the human race a big favour if they took the insides out of every pug dog and turned them into hand-warmers like those furry muffs that Russian women wear on sleighs. And another thing that makes Mr E embar-rassing to take out,* is that last time Mum did it, he stopped in front of a long bus queue and threw up on the pavement, and if that wasn't bad enough, he than ate it again in front of the same bus queue. Mum dragged him home so fast he had friction burns on his bottom.

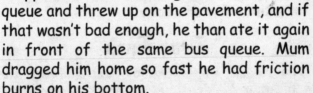

Spent rest of day at school trying to think of a better excuse for leaving the house than taking Mr E for a walk. Was so busy thinking I nearly forgot Miss Bird's detention. I had to write out one hundred times: *I must not write rude notes about my pretty teacher with the small button nose.* But because she can't read my hand-writing I wrote: *I must tell the world that my ugly teacher has a nose like a pigeon,* and she never noticed! A small victory, but a victory nonetheless.

Got home and went round to see the witch. She wasn't in so I left a note. I took Mr E with me, but wore a big peaked cap to cover my face and Mel's coat so everyone would think I was Mel if they saw me with the ugly pug. Actually, Mr E was perfectly behaved on our walk, wasn't sick once and even carried a small leaf home in his mouth, which was *nearly* sweet.

Tonight, while Mr E buried his leaf in the garden, I said my prayers for the first time since I was a baby.

# Dear Lord

*I don't usually pray, not unless I want something, and tonight I do want something. Nothing selfish, just a whopping great favour for me. Make Pamela Whitby like me. Actually I'll be honest, just 'not hating' me would be a good start. Make Pamela Whitby 'not hate' me enough to smile in my direction, even if it's a smile meant for someone behind me and I'm just sort of vaguely in the way, like a bodyguard taking a bullet for the President. Thank you Lord.*
*May the force be with you.*
*Amen etc etc etc.*

Actually no. I bet the bombs took one look at her and were so scared they went back home!

6.45 a.m. – The revenge-witch arrived! Dad's monster mum, Granny Constance, strode into the hall and slammed the door behind her. She must have had a hard life, because she looks like she disapproves of everything. Maybe she had lots of near misses by bombs in the war.

She threw off her coat and rolled up her sleeves. She was already wearing an apron underneath, and when I tried to kiss her she handed me her hat.

'Where is everyone?' she said in her clipped Irish accent. 'It's nearly seven o'clock, Alistair. Nobody ever grasped the day by rising after six thirty! Is this from you?' She smoothed out the note I'd written the night before.

'*Granary heap!* she read. '*Grinny, serve us pies. Wheel too seek and wick to log-a feet our shelves. Loo yob fat-floor-mite gruntzone, Apestir.* It must be from you. I recognize the abysmal handwriting. What does it mean?'

'It means,' I said, '*Granny, help! Granny save us please. We're all to sick and weak to look after ourselves. Love your favourite grandson, Alistair.*' She agreed to stay for one day, long enough to sort out my lazy family once and for all. Ha ha!

Went to school, but not before my personal hand *Gran*-ade had gone off with a bang.

Get it?

200

The effect she had was brilliant. She turned off tellies, opened draughty windows, cooked up semolina, force-fed castor oil, set boring puzzles and vacuumed so loudly that nobody could sleep. As I was leaving I heard her shouting up the stairs; 'Dormitory inspection at nine. I want hospital corners on all of your beds and God help you if I find one stray hair on a pillow. Lunch is *downstairs* at twelve – rollmop herrings and crispbread.'

Mel and William arrived at school at 11.45, just before lunch, having made a remarkably quick recovery from the flu.

It was lucky they hadn't arrived earlier, otherwise they'd have seen us Revengers pinning up their pictures. As it was, half the school was already laughing at them. Aaron, Ralph and I watched from behind a pillar as the crowd parted and William and Mel walked slowly towards the board where their instant *photo-larphs* were on display. Under Mel's picture we'd written: *Hi. Think I'm sexy? Then give me a call at the Dog's Home. That's 0600 655 77 856*

And we'd put William's photo under a big caption saying: WANTED: *Handsome princess to save this Sleeping Beauty! Wake me with a kiss!*

William was fighting off all the boys' kissing lips when he heard Ralph, Aaron and me snort. He and Mel gave chase. I could hear them catching up, so to make them think I was innocent, I screamed, 'It was an *accident*!'

I was hoping they'd believe me and stop, but William was already gripping the back of my collar. Luckily, that was when the five of us ran into Miss Bird, knocking her books across the corridor.

Outside the detention room, William and Mel grabbed me by the throat, pinned me up against the wall and asked if I would like to do their lines for them. Naturally, being a loving brother I said, 'Get lost, pig bums!' which I then quickly changed to 'Yes certainly, you two lovely people,' when Mel tweaked my nipples till they hurt.

But I knew that Miss Bird knew my handwriting. When we all handed our lines in, she recognized it on William and Mel's papers, as I knew she would! I was allowed to go home, while they had to sit there for another hour until they'd done their lines themselves. And fifty *extra* ones too!

When I got home Mum had recovered too. Enough to drive Granny Constance home. Apparently the older interferer had been binning Mum's precious soup bones, shouting, 'And this one's past its smell-by date too!'

Dad was crying. Mum has told him he's got a disease that hasn't been discovered yet. She looked up his symptoms in his medical encyclopaedia – always tired, addicted to rubbish TV shows, dependent on others for all his needs, an increased consumption of beer, and spilling large quantities of Tex Mex food down his pyjamas – and there was nothing listed.

AN EVENING WITH
DRAMA QUEEN
DAD

'Do you think that means I'm going to die?' he asked me.

'I hope not,' I said. More tears. Then he gave me twenty quid and told me to run down the shops and buy him a will.

'You can help me fill it in,' he said. 'It'll be good handwriting practice for you. And hurry, Alistair, or I might not be here when you get back!'

On the way to the newsagent I composed a poem on Dad dying.

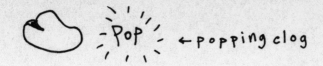

Finally I have something to say
Dad, please do not die today.
If you go and pop your clogs
Who will pay my pocket mon-ay?

Composing Dad's will was horrible. His illness has made him tired and over-emotional and he said stuff about our family that I don't need to know. Like how often he kisses Mum.

Yuck!

How gloss is that?

*To my darling wife, Miss Kiss Funny-dumpling, whose lips have shared a million puckering passions, who tickled my toes when I was ill and soothed my brow with a Wet Wipe. I leave love, memories, a house and a bank account*

I'm eleven years old. I don't want to know that someone calls my mum *Miss Kissy Funny-dumpling*. She's MY mum. She makes soup, washes clothes, shouts a lot, makes my life a misery and smells nice. That's enough.

*To my first child, Melanie, beautiful, talented Melanie. If you love your old dad half as much as he loves you, never cut your hair. Remember his pearls of wisdom on how to deal with men and you'll never go wrong in the love department: Once bitten . . . twice shy. Twice bitten . . . put a muzzle on him and chain him up in the garden.*

*I leave you lots of money. Ask your mum.*

*To my brave, clever, eldest son, William, Adonis, Apollo and a quality scrum-half too. I shall always remember your first smile that you did just for me and not for your mum as she always claimed. Ours was a special bond, William. Deep and unspoken. Father to son. Man to man. I leave you my car, my AA membership . . .*

I stopped Dad in the middle of writing this down. 'This is a will, Dad, not a book. You've just got to state facts.'

'I thought I was,' he said all hurt like a baby. 'Right. *To my youngest son, Alistair. Goodbye*

206

*and thanks for all the Christmas presents that I forgot to thank you for when I was alive. Here's a fiver.'*
Then he stopped. I waited for more.

'Is that it?' I said.

'You told me to keep it short.'

'Yeah, but you said loads of stuff about everyone else that sounded like you loved them, but you made me sound like someone you'd just met on a bus.' Now it was my turn to feel hurt and upset. I didn't care how ill my dad was he didn't deserve me. 'To my father,' I said, 'I leave you this pen so you can sign your stupid will yourself!' Then I left the room and locked myself into my bedroom, because William and Mel had just stormed in from their double detention and I did not want to be flower-pressed in the ironing board again!

During supper, I stuck close to Mum for protection. It meant I had to help her with the washing-up, but I didn't care. William splashed me with soup, and he and Mel pretended I was invisible until I spoke these words, 'Can I have some new clothes for Saturday, Mum?' I hated having to ask. If I had an allowance like the other two I could buy *what* I wanted *when* I wanted it. As it is, Mum still buys my clothes, which means that my clothes are pants whereas theirs are quality.

'What do you want new clothes for Saturday for?' asked Mel.

'Have you got a little girlfriend?' taunted William. 'Do you want new clothes to make her think you're good-looking and kiss you?'

'It's Aaron's birthday,' I said.

'Oh it's a *boyfriend*,' shrieked William. 'Alice has got a boyfriend, Mummy.'

'Lovely, darling.'

Why do mums never listen to anything we say? The only time my mum ever hears me is when I say something I don't want her to hear. Like, 'How was I to know cats got sick in tumble driers?'

'But I haven't got a boyfriend!' I shouted. 'It's not true!'

And that was when William and Mel pretended I was speaking a foreign language. 'No, sorry, Alice, can't make head nor tail of what you're saying. No comprendo. It's all gibberish.'

'I know,' said Mel, 'why don't you write down what you want to say about your boyfriend.'

'I haven't got a boyfriend!' I yelled.

'Write it down,' said William, 'or we can't

How did he know?

208

understand.'

So I wrote it down, but it didn't make any difference, because they just pretended they couldn't read my handwriting.

'*I love my boyfriend*,' read William falteringly. 'Is that what this says?'

'No!' I screamed, 'I DON'T HAVE A BOYFRIEND!' It was no good. Mel and William had got their teeth into me and weren't letting go. So I let them have it. 'One day Dad's going to die,' I said, 'and then I'll have my own money and then I'll be able to buy what I want, and what I want *won't* be *you*!' And when I looked round, Mum and Mel were crying.

'You callous brute!' shouted William. 'You've upset them now by saying Dad's going to die!'

'Dad!' bellowed Mel. 'Alice wants you to die!'

'No I don't!' I said.

'He's going to kill you!' hollered William.

I went to bed. I am never mentioning shopping again. It is a subject that inflames passions – like crutch rot.

Good night, Pamela.

Had another dream last night.

## Last Night's Dream

*Pamela and I are shopping in Knightsbridge. I've got a huge gold credit card with enough money on it to buy a boat. We're like a Playboy couple because we're both wearing dark glasses and wearing flash clothes. She's got a scarf over her expensive hair cut and I'm wearing a suit with silver buttons. And we're driving along in a red Ferrari with the roof down and she's got Mr E on her lap like one of those little dogs that really rich people have. And Mr E's been sick on her lap, but she doesn't care because she can buy another dress and anyway he's eating it up again. And we're stopping at all the flash clothes shops – CK, Hugo Boss, Armani, Man at Argos – and I go in and buy what I like and come out with tons of boxes. It's brilliant. And we turn to each other on the pavement and I say, 'Life's so much better since Dad died. We've got all the money in the world.' And we both nod at the truth, but there's one thing I'm not happy with. Everyone's suddenly pointing at me. Policemen appear from side streets and run towards me. I*

210

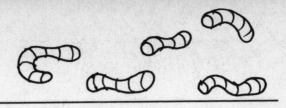

try to run away, but there's a weight on my shoulders dragging me down, and when I look back I see what I'm towing behind me – it's a lump of writhing maggots! It's Dad's dead body!

Woke in a sweat. This was William and Mel's fault for putting Dad's ghost in my head. Little niggles and jibes I can take, but messing with my head deserves payback. So, nicked Dad's will from his bedside table and changed it by crossing out what Dad had told me to write and putting in what I thought was better.

*To Mel and William I leave diddly-squat, because they're a horrid ~~brother and sis~~ children who deserve to get a good kicking.*

*To my favourite child, Alistair, I leave everything (except what Mum needs to live a comfortable life in an Old Folk's Home).*

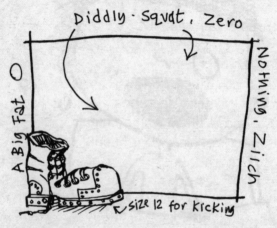

Diddly-squat, Zero

A Big Fat O

Nothing, Zilch

Size 12 for kicking

The clever bit of my plan was that it was my handwriting I was changing so the changes didn't look like changes. Well, they *did* look like changes, but changes made by the person who wrote the will in the first place, which everyone will assume was Dad. The other clever bit was remembering all the time that it was Dad writing the words not me. I spotted 'brother and sis . . .' so I can't be stupid!

# Mel

Took the will down to breakfast, where Mum was sitting with a towel over her head and her head over a large bowl of soup that she was sucking up through her nostril.

'Why don't you use a spoon?' I asked.

'Id's ad idhalation,' she said. 'Clears de tubes.'

Mel and William walked in. This was my moment. 'Look what I found upstairs,' I said cunningly. 'Dad's will. Sit down. It's going to come as a terrible shock. I'm so sorry, I thought Dad loved us all the same.' Their faces were a picture! They didn't know what they were going to hear next. 'Read it for yourselves,' I said, trying not to snigger.

If I was to take up acting as a profession, I honestly think some people would ask me to stop, because I'm so good that other actors would never get any work – except for Carol Boring-woman, Pauline Squirt, Caroline Biscuit-tin, and Trevor Macdonut who have to be in everything that's ever on TV these days. And anyway, I wouldn't be going up for their parts, would I? I'm *not* a newsreader, I'm *not* a woman and I'm *not* fat.

Mel and William couldn't read my handwriting so I had to read it to them. They listened to their fate in silence. I swear the blood drained right out of them, because when they looked up they were both as white as sheets.

'Oh dear,' said William.

'It's really tragic, isn't it?' I smirked.

'It's not funny, Alice. You're in real trouble.' This was not what I was expecting to hear. 'If Dad was to die now and you were to inherit all his money, what would the police think?'

'Murder?' suggested Mel.

'Yes,' said William. 'Youngest son gets nothing in the original will so changes it in his favour. Then bumps the old man off.'

'But I didn't,' I said. 'I mean I haven't. I won't.'

'His only mistake,' smiled Mel, 'was not disguising his very distinctive handwriting.'

'But Dad told me to do it!' I said panicking.

'But how can that be, Alice?' said William

pointing to my crossing out. 'Because we're not dad's brother and sis . . . are we? Do they still hang people for murder these days, Mel?'

'No, William, they just bang them up in a Bad Boy's Prison with axe-murderers and child-eaters. Let's hope Dad gets better, Alice, for your sake, because if he dies . . .' My big brother and sister snorted with laughter.

Suddenly felt stupid and wished I hadn't been so hasty. I didn't know it was illegal to

change a will.

'It was an *accident*,' I shouted. 'I spilled coffee over the will and it washed away the ink, all the letters and words and things; so I tried to remember what the words were and write them back in so no-one would notice, but I must have got them wrong.' Even I wasn't convinced by my story. Nor was William.

'Dead man walking,' he said. 'Dead man walking!'

I could hear my heart beating.*

I felt sick. Not even when Mum said from under the towel, 'Alistair, I *will* take you shopping. After school today. It's just what we need to put us back on our feet after this nasty flu,' could I be shaken from my fear. All I could hear in my head was the rattle and clang of a prison door!

At school, Ralph and Aaron were cross.

'You've only got yourself to blame,' said

Ralph. 'The Revengers are a team. We act *together* or not at all. You cough, I cough. He coughs, we all cough.'

'Why?' said Aaron. 'What's wrong with my cough? Why does everyone get infected by my cough and not by yours?'

'It's like the Musketeers,' said Ralph. 'Strength in numbers. I scratch your back, you scratch mine. He scratches my back, we all scratch each others' backs.'

'Now I've got fleas!' said Aaron. 'Are you saying I don't bath, Ralph?'

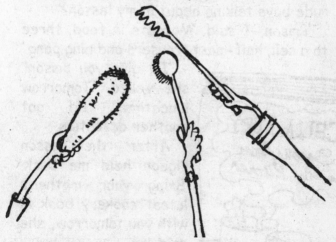

'No, I'm saying have patience. Alistair should have brought his plan to us first. We could have told him that changing a will often leads to beheaditation.'

'It was an *accident*,' I said. This was my story and I was sticking to it.

# 'QUIET!'

The pigeon was trying to explain what Chaucer meant by 'throng'. 'What are you rude boys talking about in my lesson?'

'Prison,' I said. 'Maggots in food, three to a cell, half-mast trousers and ping pong.'

'I'll give you prison!' she yelled. 'Tomorrow lunchtime!' I'd got another detention.

After the lesson Pigeon held me back. 'Bring your mother's latest cookery book in with you tomorrow,' she said.

'*Smells From a Soup Kitchen?*' I asked.

'That's it,' she said.

218

'Ridiculously priced at £25.'

I said I would when really I just wanted to know why.

At lunch, used Ralph's phone to call Dad and check he wasn't dying, but there was no reply. Had visions of him lying on the floor unable to reach the phone. Kept thinking, if he had one of those distress flares around his neck like they give to old people and round-the-world yachtsmen, he could fire red smoke into the sky and I could run back and save his life.

On the way home, tried to buy him

flares, but bizarrely the shop in which I'd seen them advertised only sold trousers.

Bought him a box of cheap chocolates instead, because that's what everyone gets in hospital to make them better.

When I got home I was greeted by Mel and William. They were standing in the hallway with long sad faces. They both kissed me and ruffled my hair and tried to force kindly smiles.

'Where's Dad?' I said nervously.

Mel looked like she was going to cry. 'He's gone . . .' she choked and couldn't finish.

'He's gone!' I shouted. 'But he can't go. It's not my fault.' I started running up the stairs, only to hear Mel finish her sentence behind me.

'He's gone . . . to the loo!' she laughed.

I banged on the door. 'Dad, are you in there?'

220

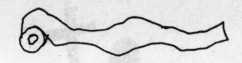

'If you're after *Golf Monthly*, you'll just have to wait,' he said.

'So you're not nearly dead?' I said. 'I've bought you stuff to make you all right again.'

'Just as well,' he said. 'I can't seem to beat this disease.'

When he came out of the loo I helped him back to bed and told him I loved him and would never do anything to harm him, and to prove it I gave him his mobile phone to keep next to him so that if ever he felt like he was dying he could call me for help.

'When did you get a mobile phone?' he said.

'What?' I said. 'I haven't got a mobile phone.'

'So how can I call you then?' I hate technology. If you're not at the cutting edge it makes you feel so inadequate. Just then Mum called. Time for shopping. In all the panic I'd forgotten.

In the hall, before we got in the car, I also told Mum that I loved Dad, so that if the police asked her if I was a murderer she'd say no.

'What is wrong with him?' I asked. 'Everyone else seems to be getting better. He's just getting worse.'

'And will do for the next two weeks,' she said.

I was horrified. 'Why? What's he got? You know something, and you're not telling us!'

'He's got two weeks of safety inspections at work,' said Mum, 'which is more hassle than he knows what to do with.'

Now I'm confused. Does that mean Dad's really ill or not ill at all?

Forgot all about Dad when I got in the car and saw Mel and William sitting in the back seat.

'What are *they* doing here?' I said to Mum. 'I thought this was a special trip – just you and me. We never spend quality time together.'

'Oh don't be ridiculous, Alistair. They asked me to come. William's got to buy something for the rugby club lunch and Mel's got a date.'

'But they've got an allowance. They can spend their money when they want to. They only want to spend it now to wreck my trip.'

'I'm not listening,' said Mum. 'This is stupid.'

I bet if she'd looked in her mirror she'd have seen them sniggering. I pulled the lever under the seat and shot backwards over William's shins.

'Ow!' he squealed.

'Sorry,' I said innocently. 'It was an *accident*!'

We drove to the shops in silence. Mum's mobile phone rang and I answered it. It was Dad checking that Mum's mobile phone was working so he could call if he needed anything.

I knew this shopping trip was going to be a disaster. I wanted to go into streetwise shops like Pin, Pukka, Pie, Rap, Rip, Tide, and Tag where all the shop assistants were young and rude, but Mum chose Thomas Brothers Department Store – *Quality Clothes at a Price that's Nice!*

'Because there's room for growth in their clothes, Alistair.'

'There's room for a wheelchair,' I muttered. 'They're for old people.'

We spent the first hour looking at black dresses for Mel. The first one she tried on looked fine and we all told her so, but she wasn't sure if it made her look fat. Mum said it didn't, but Mel is a girl and still had to try on every other black dress that had ever been made in the world, and then, just when I was hoping for a meteorite to smash up her changing room, she tried on the first one again!

'This'll do fine,' she said. I narrowed my eyes and pointed to my watch.

Next of course was William. Second oldest always goes second, which condemned me* to bottom spot. William needed something smart to pass him off as 18 in the rugby club bar. I suggested a balaclava, but nobody laughed. It took another three-quarters of an hour to decide which pair of 'stay-pressed' slacks made him look tallest and which button-down shirt made him look oldest. He chose well. In his comfortable new clothes he looks like Great Uncle Crawford's twin.

It was 5.20 when mum asked me what I wanted. The store closed in ten minutes.

'I don't know,' I said, which drew a weary chorus of 'Oh come on Alice' from my brother and sister. 'We haven't got all day to hang around here waiting for you to make up your mind.'

'All right,' I said. 'Trousers. Sexy trousers and a T-shirt with WOW on the back or something funny like that.'

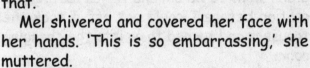

Mel shivered and covered her face with her hands. 'This is so embarrassing,' she muttered.

'Go away,' I said.

'How about these?' said Mum, picking up the nearest pair of trousers she could find. They were yellow.

'No,' I said.

'Oh come on, Alistair!' she sighed. 'There

isn't time to be fussy! If I've made the effort to bring you here, the least you can do is try them on!'

It felt like I'd been put on a train I didn't want to be on, and it was leaving the station before I could get off. I took the trousers and turned to go into the changing room.

'No, here,' Mum said. 'There's nobody around. It'll be quicker.'

'What?' She wanted me to drop my trousers in the middle of Thomas Brothers Department Store! Had she gone mad?

So there I was, scarlet with embarrass-

I think mothers do go mad, quite often actually, e.g.
spitting on handkerchiefs and rubbing the spit in your
face; picking your nose with their little finger;
squeezing your spots on a bus full of schoolgirls.

---

ment, Mel and William giggling, no trousers on and about a million shoppers staring at my down-belows, when a man with a camera approaches Mum and says he's from the local paper. 'Celia Fury? TV chef? Harold Hodges from the *Tooting Tribune*. Can I get a picture for our gossip page – *The Stars Are Out in Tooting*. Do you mind? You and your lovely family?'

And before I know what's happening, Mum's all celebrity-smile, William and Mel are cosying up for a group hug and I'm standing in the middle in my underpants!

'I don't want my photo taken like this!' I said.

'Smile, little girl,' said the photographer.

'I'm a BOY!' I said. 'I'll show you my conkers.'

'If, you don't want the photo taken,'

A I was standing there in my underpants! How many more clues did he want?

227

William whispered in my ear, 'Spoil it. Stick your finger through the front of your pants, then when they develop it they'll think it's obscene and chuck it away.'

'Do you think it'll work?'

'Of course.'

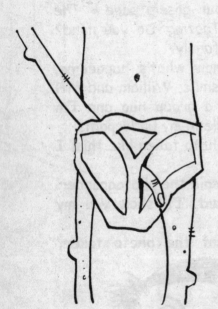

'Thanks,' I said, sticking my finger through the Y of my Y-fronts. I had misjudged William. Sometimes he could be really nice and a pleasure to be related to.

Anyway the photo was taken and then it was 5.30. I explained to Mum that I hated the yellow trousers because a) they were yellow, b) they were yellow and c) they were yellow, but she said it was them or nothing, and she hadn't come all this way just to waste her time, so yellow trousers it was. I shall never wear them, nor the matching yellow shirt she snatched off a shelf by the check-out. How can I face Pamela Whitby looking like a canary?

As we were leaving Mum's phone rang again. I answered it.

'Hello Alistair,' said Dad in a weedy voice. 'I'm still ill, so don't go telling your Mum I'm not. Thing is, normally I've just got the appetite of a little baby sparrow, but right now I could do some serious damage to a Chinese take-away and a nice bottle of cold rice wine. OK?'

I told Mum.

Outside, William and Mel burst into another fit of laughter.

'What have I done this time?' I said.

'I can't believe you actually did it!' hooted William. 'Sticking your finger through your pants! Of course they're going to publish that photo now. It's a

scoop! *Celia Fury in Sex-Mad Shopping Orgy!* The police are bound to get involved. They'll have to – it's a public indecency what you've done, Alice!'

'If it's not murder it's flashing!' said Mel. 'Do you *want* to go to prison, little brother?'

I am a depressed fugitive. And I'm never going shopping with Mum ever again. I volunteered to fetch Dad's take-away just to get away from my stupid family.

Disaster! Dad has got food poisoning from the Chinese food. We were downstairs when he rang us up from the loo to say he

230

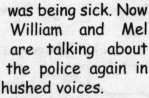

was being sick. Now William and Mel are talking about the police again in hushed voices.

'It's obvious what they're going to think,' said Mel.

'After all, you were the one who got the take-away.'

'I just fetched it,' I said. 'I didn't cook it.' But that was irrelevant apparently, because there was still plenty of time between picking the food up at the counter and getting back in the car for me to have slipped the poison in!

Wish the phone would stop ringing! First, thought it was the police, but it was just Andy for Mel. Second time, thought it might be the prison wanting to measure me up for my prison clothes, but it was Andy again. Third time, thought it might be the undertakers wanting my size for the coffin they were going to build for when I was hanged! I might have guessed it was Andy.

4.00 a.m. I have just woken from another bad dream.

## Another Bad Dream

*I'm in prison wearing yellow prison fatigues and the only visitor I get is Pamela Whitby. She's baked me a cake and as she leaves she winks and says there's something in the cake that I might like. Then I'm back in the cell, tearing the cake apart looking for a metal file to saw through my bars and all I can find is a small bottle of blue dye and a note: If you don't change the colour of your clothes I shall stop loving you.*

# FRIDAY

Knew it was going to be a bad day when I got out of bed and stepped on Napoleon, our cat. He screeched and sprang from the floor onto the window ledge. Only on account of him having no tail, he lost his balance, fell out of the window, rolled down the roof and flipped over the guttering into the garden. I thought cats were always supposed to land on their feet. So why did Napoleon land on his head in a watering can?

On way to the bathroom Mel did oh-so-funny *neenaw-neenaw* siren noises in my ear. Then she said, 'I haven't got enough space to hang up my new black dress, so I thought I'd borrow your wardrobe, OK?'

No please or thank you. She just barged into my bedroom and when I came out of the bathroom all my

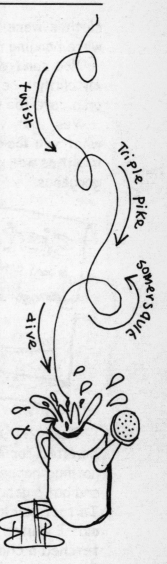

twist

triple pike

somersault

dive

233

clothes were in a heap, while all of hers were hanging neatly in my cupboard.

'You can't do that!' I said. 'What about *my* clothes getting creased? I'm going out on a date too you know.'

'Yes, but you're a boy. Nobody cares what you look like,' said Mel. 'Whereas I might as well commit suicide if I don't look gorgeous.'

'Really?' I said. 'You don't look gorgeous.' I waited for Mel to honour her words, but nothing happened, so I popped downstairs and got a good strong rope from the cellar. 'In fact you look hideous. Really puffy and old.' I waited again. Again no suicide, so I fetched a chopper from the kitchen. 'Well go on then, dog-face. Top yourself.'

Mel put the chopper on a table and stormed off. I knew her offer was too good to be true!

Just as I was leaving for school, the phone rang. It was Mrs Muttley asking why I'd missed my piano lesson again.

'I would have phoned,' I said, 'but without fingers I can't press the buttons to dial. Or pick up the phone in fact.'

'So how did you answer the phone just now?' she screeched.

'With my tongue,' I said.

'Then how can you speak?' she said. 'If you're holding the phone in your tongue?'

'My tongue's double jointed!'

'Are you lying to me?' she said.

'No,' I said. 'It's true.' She said if I was not there next week she'd take it as a personal insult. Must remember not to be there next week.

No sooner had I put the receiver down than it rung again. This time it was Dad phoning down on his mobile to see if everyone had forgotten him.

'No,' I said. 'You never forget who your dad is.'

'I meant has everyone forgotten I'm ill.'

'You sound better,' I said hopefully.

'I'm not,' he said. 'But at least that Chinese food's all out now.' I asked him how he knew. 'Water chestnuts float,' he said. 'I counted them all in and I counted them all out again.'

'So you're not going to die?' I checked.

'Only of hunger,' he replied. I made him breakfast in bed.

They do say that when you've been in bed as long as Dad has, you forget how to live with normal human beings and develop a fear of the outside world. If I was his doctor, I'd prescribe something to make him get up – like a house fire.

At school I was desperate to meet the Revengers to plan some revenge, but we couldn't get together till lunchtime and even then we had to do Pigeon's detention first. While the others did lines, she pulled me aside and asked if I'd brought my mum's new cookery book. I showed it to her.

'Good,' she said. 'I want you to start at the beginning and copy out every recipe exactly, in your neatest handwriting. And if you don't finish today, you can carry on in your next detention.'

'What next detention?' I said. 'I may never get another one in my life.'

'Oh, you will,' she said. 'Trust me.'

'Do you want me to copy out the bit on the back cover about Mum?' I said.

'No, no, no,' she snapped. 'Just the recipes. I can't cook *the bit on the back cover about Mum*, can I?'

'She just wants your mum's book free,' whispered Aaron when I sat down.

'Easy peasy revenge though,' said Ralph. 'Copy out the recipes *wrong*! Add a few nasties – chillies, and extra tablespoon of pepper, some octopus ink! She won't know whether she's coming or going.'

'She'll be going,' I sniggered, 'every five minutes!'

The bell rang for afternoon lessons before I could sort out revenges for William and Mel. We ran down the corridor towards Pigeon's classroom, but halfway there I stopped and sauntered.

'What are you doing?' shouted Ralph. 'Hurry up, or you'll get another detention.'

'I know,' I said. Ralph's revenge idea was too good to miss! Successfully secured my fourth detention in four days.*

Adjusted Mum's much-loved recipes, as follows:

*1) To the broth of steaming scallops, prawns and clams with black beans, coriander and lime, I added a handful of stinging nettles and two large chicken's feet.*

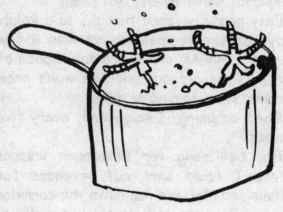

238

2) To a vegetarian soup of mung beans and fresh herbs, I added some left-over pork fat.

3) In the recipe for sweet peppers and celeriac soup, I added that old gardener's favourite - nine tablespoons of finely diced leaves.

4) And finally I gave a lift to the soup Mum had called stuffed, rolled and baked sardines with pine nuts and fresh herb soup, by adding chopped mouse to the stuffing.

Then I handed the bits of paper in to Miss Bird, pointed out that she was salivating from the corners of her mouth, and went home hoping that she was cooking tonight!

Good news, I think. Dad still can't get out of bed or cook for himself, obviously, but feels strong enough to tackle a large gin and tonic. The alcohol kills the germs apparently.

Mel has decided that she needs forty-eight hours to get ready for her Sunday date with Andy. This means she's trying on every piece of clothing she owns seven times. As all her clothes are in my bedroom, I am banished to the sitting room all night and forced to sit with a mum who thinks me ungrateful and doesn't like me. Tried tickling her toes to break the tension, but it turns out she hates that too, especially when I poke a hole in her sock.

Tried to go to bed early, but couldn't get into my room. Mel has left it in such a mess that the door won't open. Behind it is a clothes mountain. My bed is buried. I can't sleep there. When I protested to Mel she locked herself in the bathroom to stick on those long false nails that make girls look like Edward Scissorhands, and pretended she couldn't hear.

Went back downstairs and <u>slept on the</u> sofa. When I told Mum why, she said, 'Fine, I was just going to bed anyway. No sitting up late though, and no watching any naughty films.'

So that is how it is. If I am to make my own way in this big bad world I'm on my

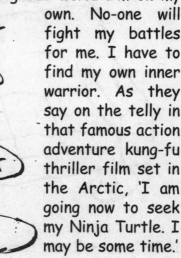

own. No-one will fight my battles for me. I have to find my own inner warrior. As they say on the telly in that famous action adventure kung-fu thriller film set in the Arctic, 'I am going now to seek my Ninja Turtle. I may be some time.'

To pay back Mum for her inconsideration I did sit up and watch a naughty film – *The Phantom of the Opera*. It was the most terrifying thing I have ever seen. I had hairs sticking

I was expecting her to tell Mel off with a big beating stick

241

up on the back of my neck, goosebumps, sweaty armpits, the works! When Mr E nudged open the sitting room door and Napoleon leapt onto my shoulders like a huge hairy hand, I actually screamed and jumped off the sofa. Lasted ten minutes before I switched the whole thing off. Why does anyone watch scary movies? They're *scary*.

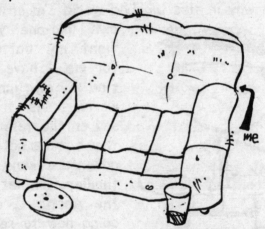

me

11.30 p.m. – I am completely awake and think I might be mad. Outside our house there is ghostly piano music playing. I can hear a spooky piano tinkling through the wall. This is like what happened in the *Phantom* film. If I am shortly to become a grisly victim of the loopy piano-playing madman in the sewers, I really hope he doesn't kill me to the tune of *Super Trouper* by Abba, because that is Mrs Muttley's favourite tune and I'd hate to die thinking of her!

Now that I'm awake, I cannot believe that I have got through a whole day without thinking up good revenges on Mum, William and Mel, especially after what they have done to destroy my life! I phoned Ralph's mobile to pick his brains for evil ideas. But when the phone was answered, it wasn't Ralph. I know, because I said, 'Marmalade cats like cream,' and a gruff voice said, 'Tooting Police, can I help you?'

Brain picking!

I slammed the phone down in a panic. How had that happened? I might have misdialled, but what if I'd pressed redial by mistake? What if someone else had been phoning the police earlier? What if Dad was dead and I was about to be arrested?

243

Ran upstairs to check on Dad. He wasn't dead. He was snoring like an elephant seal and Mum was sleeping next to him with a tissue in either ear. She looked like she had one long tissue pulled right through her head.

So why had I called the police? Was it a mistake or was it guilt? Was I ready to confess or was I somehow inside an episode of the *X Files*? And why was the piano outside now playing *Super Trouper* by Abba? Is that not the most spooky coincidence you ever heard?

Tried to get back to sleep, but the house wouldn't let me. All those creaks and sighs and groans and squeaks turned my head into a blender. I imagined ghouls and ghosts lurking in the shadows waiting to chop me up! And every two minutes Mr E crashed through the cat flap and Napoleon went to sleep and fell off the back of the sofa. Between cat thump and cat flap I was in a state of nervous tension, and not even thinking angelic thoughts about Pamela Whitby could break this cycle of fear!

I passed a restless night.

# SATURDAY

Was half-woken by the local paper dropping through the letterbox. Was fully
woken by the front page. A picture of me
with my finger poking through my pants
and a headline that said: **WHO'S A WILLY LITTLE
BOY THEN!**

This humiliation is William and Mel's
fault. I don't
care what the
Revengers
said    about
patience.    I
can no longer
wait    for
revenge!

THE TOOTING WORLD

**WHO'S A WILLY
LITTLE BOY THEN?**

CONKERS

FAINTED

Mum and
Dad never
eat   sugar,
not even in
tea.    But
my    big
brother and
sister do. So I crept into the
kitchen where somehow the sugar got
knocked into the dustbin *by accident* and
the bowl was refilled with salt.

The doorbell rang. It was Granny
Constance, waving her copy of the local

I am still cleverly writing 'by a
', in case this diary should fall into enemy hands. Then
cannot be blamed for anything, because 'by accidents, which are nobody's fault!

245

paper and shouting for Mum.

'It's eight o'clock in the morning!' she said, as Mum stumbled downstairs. 'It's practically the afternoon. Are you abandoning your children to bring *themselves* up, Celia?'

'Yes,' I said. 'It's a miracle we're normal.' Granny raised the rolled up newspaper and hit me on the legs. 'Ow!' I said. 'That hurt!'

'It was meant to,' she said. 'If I had my way I'd bring back the birch!'

'You'll feel better after a nice cup of tea,' Mum said. And she took Granny into the kitchen while I rubbed my bruises.

Suddenly I realized what she'd said.

'NO!' I shouted. 'NOT A CUP OF TEA!' I rushed into the kitchen just as Mum was spooning three spoons of salt into the old dragon's cup.

'Why not?' said Mum. 'Tea never killed anyone.'

'Here let me help you,' I said, grabbing Granny's cup and *by accident* chucking it out of the window. 'Oh dear and that was our last tea bag,' I said.

'No it wasn't,' said Mum.

'I meant tea . . . pot,' I said, sliding the teapot off the table and *by accident* smashing it on the floor. 'That was our last teapot.'

'The boy has finally gone mad,' said Granny Constance.

'He's got a date this afternoon,' said Mum, as if that explained my behaviour, 'with a **G-I-R-L**.'

'Oh,' said Granny. 'That's the **E-N-D** of him then!'*

The phone rang and Granny answered it. 'It's the invalid,' she snapped to Mum. 'He

oooops

says he hasn't been fed yet, Celia. Must I do everything in this house?'

She took up Dad's breakfast and showed him the paper. He immediately summoned his family to his bedside.

'Alistair,' he sighed, as he took his cup of tea from Granny. 'Alistair, Alistair, Alistair . . .'

'Good morning, Daddy,' I said, while Mel smiled slyly.

'Alistair's a very naughty boy, isn't he?' she said.

Dad shook his head sadly and took a sip of his tea. That was the end of the lecture. His face went purple, the cup tipped over and boiling water splashed hotly down his front.

'What was that?' he howled.

'Hot tea with milk and sugar,' said Granny.

'He doesn't take sugar,' said Mum.

'Poison!' said William. 'Alistair's trying to kill him.'

'Don't be daft,' I replied. 'It was salt, meant for you two.'

Mum called an ambulance while Dad sent me to my room, but I couldn't get in because of Mel's clothes, so I stood on the landing like a lemon, not knowing what to do. I was still there when Dad was carried past on the stretcher.

'I'm not disobeying you,' I said. My voice was trembling. I felt really guilty about the salt in his tea. 'It's Mel's clothes, they're blocking the door.'

'Then clear them up,' he howled through gritted teeth. I felt so bad I did as I was told. And that's why I spent my morning – when I should have been getting ready for a hot date with Pamela Whitby – picking up and folding Mel's clothes!

Meeting Aaron in front of the cinema at 1.30. At 12.30 hid my yellow clothes inside the Scalextric box underneath my bed. Then instead of my canary suit put on my favourite jeans, favourite jumper and favourite trainers. Crept downstairs and had just opened the front door when Mel stepped out of the sitting room, where she'd obviously been waiting all week to ambush me. Then in a voice that was loud

249

enough for Dad to hear in the hospital burns unit, she screamed, 'Are you going now then, Alistair? Mummy's seen the way you're dressed has she?'

Death is too good for her! But flesh-eating scarab beetles burrowing through her body till they eat out her heart would go someway to making me feel better!

Mum sent me back to my room to change. I told her I couldn't find my yellow clothes, but William suggested I look inside the Scalextric box underneath my bed. Thank you, William.

When I was finally dressed, I stood in front of the mirror and was *maniacally* depressed. You know that numb feeling you get when you're standing in the middle of the road and a building's falling on your head and above you there's a jumbo jet about to crash and underneath your

feet there's an earthquake? Well, that's what I felt like. Picked on. I looked like a chicken drowning in custard.

Granny C + = ♡PAMELA♡

The disapproving look on Pamela Whitby's face when she saw my yellow clothes was everything I knew it would be. She looked just like Granny Constance sucking a lemon, only with more teeth. It turned out she'd also seen my candid photo in the *Tooting Tribune*. She hadn't wanted to come because of it. Apparently, she had strict rules about never associating with male strippers who showed their winkies in magazines, but she'd bought a new dress for the occasion so she had to come.

'And thank you, Alistair, for not saying how pretty I look in it,' she said.

'No problem,' I replied. She'd said thank you. Maybe I wasn't doing so badly after all!

'I didn't mean it,' she said.

'But I thought . . .'

'Anyone who thinks that the finger-willy thing is still funny when they're eleven is too immature for me,' she said.

'But it was my brother,' I told her.

'Ugh! You let your brother poke his finger out of your pants,' she said. 'Gross! You're even more of a disgustingly sick person than I thought you were earlier!'

That was in the foyer.

In the cinema, Ralph and Aaron kept winking at me and playing seat-frog until they managed to get Pamela Whitby and me sitting next to each other. But as the lights went down, my yellow clothes started glowing in the dark. I looked like a radioactive banana. I passed Pamela Whitby a note, saying: I apologize for my appearance. Will never happen again.

But because of my bad hand-

252

*From what I could hear, it was called **Doctor Voodoo** and was all about a snake-worshipping sect in Tahiti who took revenge on a wicked developer, who was trying to get them off their island, by scaring him with ancient woodland curses and voodoo black magic.

writing she read it as: *I assume both your parents were hippopotamuses.* So I got a slap round the ear, which meant I couldn't hear a word of the film.*

And Pamela Whitby turned her back on me and sighed with irritation everytime I looked at her.

After the film, I called a meeting of the Revengers in the gents loo. 'Marmalade cats like cream,' I said. 'Friends, you've got to help me! These last two days have been torture! My life is pants! I must have revenge.'

We looked up to see a man standing behind us. 'Sorry,' he said. 'I thought . . .'

I stepped forward. 'This loo is closed,' I said, 'by order of the police.'

'And we are the police,' said Ralph.

'CID,' said Aaron.

'What does that mean then?' he said.

'Child Investigation Department,' said Ralph.

'We're an anti-children crime squad,' I said, 'who check out small windows in public places to see if children can crawl through them to commit crime. Five minutes and we'll have the whole case sewn up!'

'Well get a move on,' he said. 'I'm busting.'

When we were alone again I listed my
grievances.

1) Mum's betrayal on the yellow
   trouser front causing the Pamela
   Whitby slapping incident.
2) No grown-up allowance.
3) The embarrassing naked-finger
   photo.
4) Mel and William for being born.
5) The whole police threat thing
   that my big brother and sister
   had made happen with my
   rewriting *by accident* of Dad's
   will.

'There's a bounty on my head,' I said. 'I'm
a wanted man.'

'Not by Pamela Whitby!' snorted Ralph. I
ignored this wounding comment and asked
the big question instead. What could we
do?

'Voodoo,' said Aaron.

When we left the loo there was a queue
of embarrassed men hopping up and down in
the corridor. They all had damp trousers.

Dad is home from hospital. The doctor says

254

he needs a few days in bed to recover from the shock. Dad is taking it rather well. He's opened a bottle of champagne and is lying in bed, singing. He called me in. 'Thanks to your scalding,' he said, 'I really *can't* be there!'

'Where?' I said.

'Never you mind,' he laughed. 'Good work, son!' Then he gave me a huge kiss.

Kissing men is like kissing Mr E – stinky, wet and bristly. Kissing women however is like kissing warm jelly. I think I must be a jelly man. Only not with Granny Constance, because kissing Granny Constance is like kissing a bristly jelly made with antiseptic floor wash.

2.15 a.m. – Woken up by more spooky piano music outside my bedroom window.

Suddenly thought it might be Pamela Whitby trying to make up for her stand-offishness today by serenading me under my window. Rushed to window and flung open curtain, but Pamela Whitby wasn't there. The music stopped too, and a car drove off with no lights. Spent the next twenty minutes trying to re-hang curtain on its rail.

It has not been my best day. Sometimes I wish I lived in an igloo on my own with no family, no girls, and no clothes.

Except for a warm seal-skin jumper. One that was clubbed humanely obviously.

I hate fish I really do

Just penguins – simple creatures with no axe to grind, simple flightless birds content with their lot of ice, fish and snow.

Nice

# zzzZZZZUNDAY

I need my bedroom to myself. In one hour I am creating voodoo revenge magic against my evil family.

I knocked on Mel's door with my arms full of folded clothes. 'It's Sunday,' I shouted, but she was still asleep. I could hear her turning over in bed. 'You've got a date with Andy today.'

In a flash she was at the door in her pyjamas.* 'Oh brilliant,' she said, drowsily. 'Thanks for waking me, Alistair. I was meant to get up an hour ago to paint my nails.' She wasn't going to start being *nice* to me now, was she? She took her clothes with a smile and said, 'Thanks.' She *was*! I couldn't believe it. It wasn't fair! She couldn't suddenly be nice to me just as I was lining up the revenge of a lifetime!

So I tried to make her cross by shouting, 'Take your ugly black dress as well, you fat cowpat!' And threw the dress in her face, because I wanted her to hate me again so I could do evil things unto her without feeling guilty. But she was too fast asleep.

'Sorry,' she said. Then, 'Thanks again, Alistair.'

*That's not a door in her pyjamas she'd never get any sleep because people would be opening and closing the door all night. Unless it was a revolving door of course, but that wouldn't be much better, because you can trap your fingers in those.

That's at the door w

> If she'd had a door in

*Actually it's not my razor she uses, it's Dad's, but it sounds better if I say mine. And anyway I already have shaved once with hardly any blood, so it's only going to be a few weeks before I'm shaving full time.

# BIG SISTERS!

You can't trust them to be nice
and you can't trust them
to be nasty.

The only thing you
can trust them to do is use
your razor to shave their legs!*

This morning, Dad had a hangover, but was still well-chuffed with his burns. 'A week off at least,' he grinned, as he waved William off to his rugby. 'Good luck, son, and remember, set and drive, half-breaks, and don't forget to shout from one to ten before kick-off. That's where the game's won. I'm proud of you!' He was crying when he turned round. Sport did that to him. He couldn't play it, but he sure could cry about it. When I called him a cry-baby, he looked quite upset and said it was the blisters rubbing against his bandages.

The Revengers arrived, and I impressed

bottom gas

on them the need to get our skates on where striking back was concerned. So after we'd hung a sign on the bedroom door that said

# ENTER AT YOUR PERIL

## - CURRIED EGG EATING CONTEST -

## LETHAL GAS LEAK

we got straight down to it. Or rather we would have done if Mel hadn't suddenly burst in.

'You little toad,' she screamed. 'Look at the creases in my black dress! If I'm not ready for Andy when he comes you'll pay big time. Every time you're in the loo for the next five years I'll switch off the light! I hate you, Alice! I wish you'd never been born! And I'm *not* a fat cowpat!' She slammed the door as she left.

The other two Revengers were shocked at what she'd said, but I was delighted. 'Everything's back to normal,' I said, rubbing my hands. 'Shall we proceed with the punishment?'

We decided to make three voodoo dolls. 'How do we do that?' said Aaron.

'I don't know,' I said. 'It's a shame they never made voodoo dolls on *Blue Peter*, isn't it?' I stood up to demonstrate. '*Hello, children. Today we're making a fully-working, black magic voodoo doll. And all you'll need is a used washing-up liquid bottle, an old sock, the evil eye of Schamane, some sticky-back plastic and a dozen ordinary pins. Can you do voodoo? Let's find out!*

'But that's brilliant,' said Ralph. 'That *is* how we do it.'

We found some old stuff in the bin in the kitchen and assembled it back in my bedroom. Mum's doll had a squeezy bottle for a body, pipe-cleaners for arms and legs, an old tennis ball for a head and string for hair. Then we painted **MUM** on the front so we wouldn't get muddled.

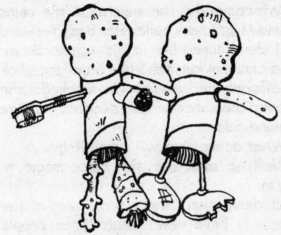

The bodies of Mel and William's dolls were made from old loo rolls. Their heads were potatoes. One of Mel's legs was a carrot while the other was an asparagus. Her arms were a toothbrush and one of Granny's half-smoked cigars. William's arms were Peperamis and his legs were the glass stems from two broken wineglasses.

Then for the magic. I wanted Mum to be less mean with her money and give me more, so we put three pennies in an Action Man saddlebag and hung it round her neck. William and Mel's punishment was less specific. I just wanted to cause them pain generally, so we stuck six sewing pins into their potatoes and loo rolls.

Unfortunately, the weight of the coins around Mum's neck pulled her body forward until she stooped like an old woman. So we put a pencil in her hand like a walking stick to support her weight. It worked. She stopped bending at 45 degrees to the perpendicular.

'What do we do now?' asked Ralph.

'Wait,' I said. 'For the black magic to kick in.'

Suddenly, there was a scratching at the door. You have never seen three people jump out their skins like we did. We thought it was an evil spirit or a gremlin at the very least, but the fur we saw flash through the door belonged to Napoleon. He padded across the floor ignoring us in that superior nose-in-the-air way he has. Then, to our horror, he jumped up onto the desk where the dolls were standing. I could see it coming. A clumsy landing, two paws up in the air whoompf! Napoleon fell over, taking William and Mel's dolls with him. Mel's doll was lucky. It just fell head first into a mug of cold, milky tea, but William's doll rolled off the desk and smashed one of its legs on the floor.

'Oops!' I said. 'What have we done?'

The doorbell rang and we found out.

It was William. He was still wearing his rugby kit. In his hands he had two crutches. On his leg a white plaster! 'It's a hairline fracture of my ankle,' he said in a tiny tearful voice. 'I've never been injured before.'

I turned to the Revengers.

# Spoooooky!

Because of William's leg, Aaron and Ralph were sent home and lunch was delayed until 4.00. This sent Mel into a tizz, because Andy was picking her up in his passion-wagon at 5.30. And because she was in her new black dress, full make-up, coiffed-up hair and tights and jewellery and everything she couldn't possibly help to carry, or serve, or talk, or pass the mustard, or do anything human, really. She was a bag of bad-tempered nerves, who got away with being rude, because as Mum said, 'It's a very stressful night for her.'*

Anyway, neither Mel nor William could walk, so Muggins had to do all the fetching from the kitchen. I don't know what happened. One moment the jug of milk was safely in my hand the next I was flying. I screamed, 'Look out!' As Mel turned to see

what I was shouting about, the milk jug dumped its load in her face. The milk soaked her hair, poured down her neck and covered her little black dress in a big white stain. The silence was electric. I couldn't move, Mel couldn't move, William couldn't move and Dad was upstairs in bed.

Mum reacted first. She picked me up by the seat of my pants and said, 'You stupid

264

selfish little boy!'

'It was an accident!' I cried. They didn't believe me. 'No it was, this time it was! I really *didn't* mean to do it. A huge ghostly hand pushed me in the back and I tripped. Honestly it did!'

The doorbell rang and Mel snapped out of her trance. She burst into tears and ran out the room dripping milk. 'I don't want to see him!' she wailed. So Mum had to tell Andy that Mel was sick and I was sent to my room again. I wouldn't have minded if I'd done it deliberately, but I hadn't. Something supernatural had pushed me!

# Double-spooooky!

But back in my bedroom I saw something that made my heart stop in terror. The pencil had slipped out of pipe cleaner and gravity had done its worst on the washing-up liquid bottle. Mum's doll was bent double. Her head was touching her knees! What in the name of the sacred jujube tree was going to happen to *her*?

Heard a scraping behind me and turned in a panic. A note had been pushed under my door.

> This is war. And like you, war is ugly. We will not be taking prisoners.
>
> M+W

Suddenly, there was a scream from downstairs. With my heart in my mouth, I rushed into the kitchen to find Mum bent double over the washing-up.

'I've put my back out,' she cried, 'picking up this pencil!'

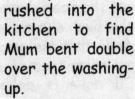

# Triple-spooooky!

Had another weird dream.

## My Another Weird Dream

*My dad dies of slothfulness. He's attacked in bed by a sloth and smothered to death. But a witch doctor wearing Mel's little black dress raises Dad from the dead with a glass of milk so he can point out his murderer. He points to me. And suddenly I realize I'm standing in a courtroom in a big furry sloth costume and the judge is Mum with a tennis ball head. Then Mel and William stand up in the dock wearing army uniforms, and promise to fight Alice Fury till he acknowledges them as superior beings with more right to breathe air than him. And the judge seems pleased, only it's not the judge anymore, it's Granny Constance waving a bunch of twigs, and she tells me to bend over and pull down my trousers . . .*

That was when I woke up. I'm awake now and can hear the house breathing again. Those dreaded noises of the night. Cracks and creaks and scrapes and squeaks and gurgling groans like the Devil. Am I going mad, dear diary? If someone up there thinks this is funny, I've got news for you, mate – it's not!

267

# MONDAY

Today has been the freakiest day of my life. It started this morning. Strange goings-on had been going on all night. The clothes I'd put away for Mel had been thrown out of her cupboard onto the landing. She blamed me, but why would I want to do all that picking up and folding again? Dad's will was stolen from William's room,* put into an envelope and left on the hall table addressed to the police. And Napoleon the tail-less cat walked along the banisters *without* falling off!

In the First Year loos at school, I shared my worst fears with the Revengers. 'We've stirred up evil,' I said. 'We've opened the black magic box and now we can't close it again!'

'No,' said Ralph. 'It's Mel and William mucking about, trying to scare you.'

'No, it can't be,' I said. 'William

*where he'd been hiding it in case he needed to blackmail me.

268

can't move anywhere unless he's on crutches and they make a thumping noise so I'd have heard him!'

'It can't be real, because they weren't real voodoo dolls,' said Aaron. 'They were made out of rubbish.'

'But I've seen the miracle with my own eyes. Guys! For once, Napoleon *didn't* fall of the banisters. He's cured! He can walk again!'

When we left the loos after the meeting there was a line of First Years waiting to go.

'Oh my God!' I gasped.

'What?' said the others.

'There!' I said, pointing to the freaky dryness. 'No wet trousers! That proves it!' Aaron and Ralph nodded their heads and smiled at me like doctors do just before they strap you into a straitjacket!

But the worst was yet to come. When I got home Dad was out of bed. Him and Mum were waiting in the kitchen. As I shut the front door they called me through, and with her walking frame, Mum pointed to her new shiny copper hood. Scratched across the front with a nail, in shaky letters 50 cm high, was the word

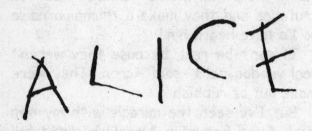

'I didn't do it,' I squeaked.

'Then who did?' seethed Mum. 'It's *your* name.'

'It's not my name! I'm not called Alice. I'm Alistair. I'm a boy. I didn't do it!'

'Fifteen hundred pounds!' exploded my dad, clutching his burns. 'Now you've gone and burst my blisters again, you stupid boy!'

'It must be them,' I said, as Mel and William walked in. 'Tell them you did it.'

My big brother and sister looked at each other and laughed.

'Why would we do this?' said Mel. 'Maybe it's the ghost!'

'What ghost?' said Mum.

The blood drained from my face. 'The ghost I keep hearing every night,' I whispered. Had Mel heard it too?

270

Then suddenly,

# CRASH!

The back door burst open and Mr E was standing outside with his front paws and face plastered black with mud. He took one look at me, yelped, bit my hand and charged outside like he'd just been stung on the bum by a bee.

'Dog's are sensitive to spirits,' said Mel. 'Did anyone else hear Mr E howling at the moon last night?'

'Me,' said William, 'at midnight when the beasts of Beelzebub scavenge for souls!'

'Stop it!' said Mum. 'You're scaring Alistair.'

'No they're not,' I lied.*

'Well, if you're petrified tonight, Alistair, I'm only next door,' said Mel. 'All you have to do is scream . . . if the bogeyman hasn't slit your throat first!'

Mum sent all three of us to bed. She's bad-tempered because of her back. Mind you, if I had to smell my cheesy feet all day I think I might be bad-tempered too. I've

straightened her doll. Let's hope it works.

4.00 a.m. – I haven't slept a wink. This house is throbbing with supernatural phenomena. I've heard clanking chains, thumping footsteps, mournful wailing, ghostly laughter and a wettish sort of splattering in the garden! Why did I do this? If I get out of this alive I shall never do revenges ever again.
Well maybe one or two

I've only gone and summoned up the dark demons of Ghede and got us haunted!

What was that noise? There was a knocking on my wall! There's something *in* there behind the wallpaper! It's only a matter of time before that door bursts open and a wild-haired, sabre-toothed thing with a hound's head and a goat's body snatches me into the fiery pits where I'll roast in Hell for time everlasting!
I wonder if Mum depriving me of food by sending me to bed without supper has affected my brain?

Is liver the most disgusting meat ever invented?

Mum woke me up. She has doubled in size since last night, but do I get thanked?

Scared to come out of my bedroom. Expecting to see blood up the walls and severed limbs stuck to the carpet, but when I did venture out it wasn't as nasty as that. The loo has been vandalized. The chain is missing. We have passed a hose pipe through the window so that we can flush at our convenience.

While we were in the garden sorting the hose I couldn't help noticing that the lawn was covered in bones. Mr E thought he'd died and gone to Heaven. 'Where do these come from?' I said.

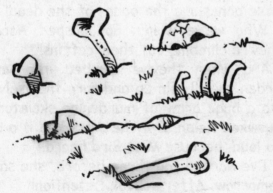

'From inside our bodies,' said William. 'Have you never heard of bones? They join together to make a skeleton.'

273

'Ha ha!' I said. 'I'm not stupid.'

'Oh sorry,' he said. 'I thought you were.'

'I meant, how did they get on the grass?'*

Later at school, Aaron pointed to the ground with a shaking finger and said softly, 'I know where the bones came from.' We all looked down. Then we all looked up again with eyes as wide as saucers. The end of Aaron's nose was twitching. 'Who's seen the film *Poltergeist*?' he trembled.

'You don't mean . . .' Ralph didn't dare say it, but I did.

'My house is built on a graveyard? So those bones are the bones of the dead!'

'Who we've woken up!' gasped Aaron. 'They're climbing out their coffins!'

And when they've climbed into your garden they'll join up and turn themselves into a huge army of murdering skeletons!' squawked Ralph. Only he squawked it a bit too loud, because Miss Bird heard.

'I've warned you three before,' she said. 'Tomorrow. After school. Detention!'

eat. It would fall off your fork all the time, being as it is, the size of a rat's dropping. I should add that if he brain was any bigger he would not be allowed to play rugby.

---

There was only one way to find out if my house was built on top of a graveyard full of zombies.

12.00 a.m. midnight – I put a handkerchief across Mr E's yappy mouth and tied him to the fridge. Aaron and Ralph were waiting for me in the garden. We all had torches and spades, although Aaron's was a plastic one from a beach set.

'We don't have a garden,' he said. 'Mum grows carrots in a window box, but she doesn't need a spade for that.'

'How many carrots do you get in a window box?' I asked.

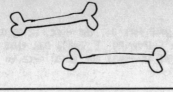

'Three,' he said. 'Small ones. I must have dug them up too soon, but I wanted to see how they were growing.'

Ralph produced a bottle of lemonade, only it wasn't lemonade. 'It's holy water,' he said. 'I nicked it out the bird bath in the garden. Before we start we've got to splash it all over to protect us from the buried-bad-things.'

We splashed the water all over our faces and hands and everywhere else by mistake. 'Has anyone got a towel?' asked Aaron. But we hadn't, so we dug wet.

1.00 a.m. – We were exhausted. We'd dug so many little holes in the lawn that they'd joined up into one large one. We found a few things from the house that Mr E had buried, like Mum's glasses, a pink sock and the TV remote, but no graveyard. It was a relief in one way but a worry in another. We still didn't know what was causing all this spookiness.

2.00 a.m. – Back in bed.

3.00 a.m. – I am never sleeping ever again! Half an hour ago, a figure appeared at the end of my bed. I couldn't see his face because he was wearing a hood, but he had something in his hand. It was a long pole that he thumped on the ground when he walked.

It was only after he'd been there a few seconds that I realized who it was. It was Death, the Grim Reaper and the thumping was his wooden scythe that he uses to harvest souls! His voice rattled like he was speaking through a paper and comb, but because this was Death I knew I was just imagining that. He said, 'Now you're for it, Alice Fury. Sleeping bones should be left to lie, but you wouldn't. Don't go to sleep tonight or you'll never wake up again!'

*or should I say ~ ~*

I screamed so loud that Death ran away, but nobody came to my rescue. I fled into Mum and Dad's bedroom, but he was snoring and she had more tissues in her ears. I thought parents were supposed to be loving and protective.*

277

# WEDNESDAY

Bit of trouble this morning when Mum and Dad opened their curtains. Their precious lawn had mysteriously vanished. In its place was a crater.

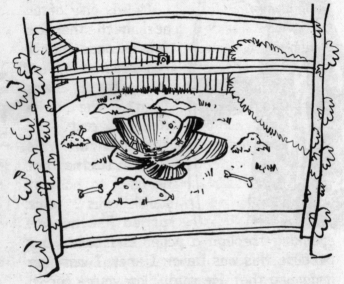

'Who did this?' wept Dad. 'I'm trying to get better here. Trying to get back to work to support my family. Then this comes along, and I think what's the point?'

'You're upset,' I said. 'Sit down.'

'I'm not upset,' Dad shouted. 'I'm angry, Alistair. Who could have done this to us?'

'Moles?' I said. 'I've heard that moles like a good party.'

'This mess is not moles partying,' said Dad coldly.

'A spaceship?' I suggested. 'As it lands, the blast from its rocket blows a hole in your lawn.'

'So where is this spaceship then?' asked William. He makes things worse deliberately. He loves watching me squirm. If he'd just let me lie without butting in everything would be all right!

'The spaceship is in another garden,' I said. 'It probably bounced on landing.'

'This is not a blast from a spaceship,' said Dad. 'This is digging.'

'Then maybe it's Mr E,' I said. 'It's not me. In fact I'm sure it's Mr E, because I found these in the kitchen this morning,' and I produced the glasses, the sock and the remote. That did the trick. They believed me.

But here's the problem – *I* know it's not true! Just as I know what *is* true; i.e. the bones, the rattling chains, the thumping walls and the Grim Reaper! I'm cursed!

'All houses make noises,' Mum said when I told her what I was scared of. 'Pipes clang, radiators gurgle, floorboards creak. That's what you're hearing.'

---

'Or maybe not,' said Mel. 'Maybe all this spookiness is something to do with Dad's illness,' she went on. 'Maybe what he was coughing up last week was ectoplasm. Maybe that's why he can't get better, because this ghost is feeding off his brain and as Dad gets weaker the ghost gets stronger, until finally Dad pops his clogs and the ghost takes his place!'

At the thought of Dad's skull being sucked inside out, I freaked. I ran down the stairs screaming. I ran out the front door screaming. I ran down the road screaming. And I only stopped screaming when I fell over a pushchair and squashed a marrow with my knee.*

'Sorry,' I said. 'I'm being chased by a ghost!'

The woman recognized my uniform and

280

reported me to the school. Got another detention to go along with the one I already had. When Miss Bird turned up to supervise me I asked her if I could do both together.

'With pleasure,' she said. 'There's nothing I like better than a double detention.'

'Me neither,' I said. I didn't tell her I was too scared to go home.

Before I could start writing out Mum's recipes I just *had* to ask. 'Did you taste any of the recipes I copied last time?' I said.

'I did,' she said. 'And how were they?'

'Delicious,' she said. Delicious! Stinging nettles, chicken's feet, pork fat, leaves and mouse! She must have taste buds like steel rivets!

'Yes, delicious,' she said. 'I found one

But then I always thought she was a robot.

281

or two of the ingredients hard to read because of your handwriting but I worked them out in the end.' She handed me the recipes I'd copied out last time. The page was full of her corrections.

~~a handful of stinging nettles~~
*a handful of steaming noodles*
~~two large chicken's feet~~
*two large chicory roots*
~~left-over pork fat~~
*left-over port wine*
~~nine tablespoons of finely chopped leaves~~
*nine tablespoons of finely diced leeks*
~~chopped mouse~~
*chocolate mousse*

So there it was. She couldn't read my handwriting. All that cunning work for nothing. But there again, if she couldn't read what I'd written it didn't matter what I wrote. So this time I went mad and in amongst the recipes I hid the following ingredients: the cremated remains of a beloved pet; a litre of virgin engine oil; curdled cream scraped from the dustbin; chipmunk wee; frog spawn; six tablespoons of ear wax; a plate of unwashed socks; half a centipede and the gunk-encrusted toe jam from a tortoise.

Got home late to find Mel and William waiting for me in the sitting room with a woman called Talia. She was all earrings and red hair. Her green dress had swirly patterns on and matched the rug in the hall.

'Oh, you're a boy,' she said. 'I thought your sister said your name was Alice.'

'I have conkers,' I said. 'Why were you talking to my sister?'

'She thinks you might be causing the hauntings,' she said. 'But be not afraid, for I am here to help.'

Talia was a psychic medium. She went into a trance to find out why we were being haunted. It was like watching a cow with BSE. She shook her head, waved her arms, fell down and foamed at the mouth. Then suddenly, she rolled back her eyes and said in a voice that was clearly not her own,* 'Hello. I'm a ghost and I've got a message for Alice . . . stair, I mean.'

Everyone gasped. How had the ghost known my name?

Talia suddenly snapped out of her trance and wiped the foam off her chin. 'Well that clearly indicates a presence, Alistair, but I'm not surprised because psychic disturbance is always channelled through the youngest boy in a family, which is you.'

'And the cure?' asked Mel.

'An exorcism,' said Talia. 'An exorcist must be found forthwith. Ooh, hang on!' Suddenly her eyes snapped shut again. 'I'm getting something else,' she said. 'Oh no! No, it can't be!'

'What?' I said.

'Death!' she shouted. 'Death! Death! Death!' She made such a racket that Mum and Dad rushed in. 'I see imminent Death in the family!' Dad immediately assumed it was him and had a fit.

'It's me, isn't it?' he wailed. 'I *am* going to die! I *am* going to die!'

And all I could think about was that stupid will! 'And I'm going to prison!' I screamed.

The room fell silent. 'Why?' said Mum and Dad together. 'What have you done now?'

Before I could answer, the phone rang. Great Uncle Crawford is dead.

When I first heard the news I jumped up and down and hugged Dad, and both of us cheered, because it *wasn't* Dad who was dead! But then we remembered that Great Uncle Crawford *was* dead, which was very sad, so we started acting sorry and trying to cry, even though neither of us produced a single tear.

I know why I couldn't cry. We're going to Ireland tomorrow for the funeral on Friday. That means I'm missing my piano lesson again! Hallelujah!

When I say *we're* going to Ireland, that's everyone except Dad. He says the shock has made his scald worse, and besides he read somewhere that flying can make a sick man explode.

'Don't worry about me,' he croaked. 'I'll

stay behind and try to get better all on my own.'

That mean's he's going to drink beer again. And Mum knows it. I can tell from her tight lips.

When Mum's mouth is pinched it looks exactly like Napoleon's bottom

Have never seen a dead body before. In Ireland they don't have lids on their coffins, because when they throw a party for the dead person they want the corpse to be able to get up and dance. If that happens while I'm in the room, I'm on the first plane home.

286

# THURSDAY

Before we left for Ireland, Mum phoned Miss Bird and said I wouldn't be in for the next couple of days.

'That's fine,' said Miss Bird, 'but tell Alistair that his punishment is Saturday morning detentions, starting this weekend, for as long as it takes till he's finished the recipes.'

'Finished the recipes?' said Mum.

'I mean caught up with his lessons,' said Miss Bird. 'Sorry! Soup of the tongue.'


Did I not swear I would never go shopping with my mum again?

We got to Heathrow airport and she said, 'Did you bring a suit?'

I said, 'No.'

'Why not?' she shrieked.

'I don't own one,' I said.

'Everyone wears a suit to a funeral,' she said, and before I could complain she'd dragged me into the nearest men's store, pulled a black suit off the peg and told me to drop my trousers.

'I won't do it,' I said. 'Look at the trouble I got into last time. If you want me to try that suit on, I'm doing it in the changing room.'

'Fine,' she hissed, 'but hurry up or we'll miss the plane.'

Felt safer in the cubicle. It had a floor-to-ceiling curtain. Not that it made any difference. I was wearing the suit jacket and had just dropped my jeans to put the trousers on, when I heard a loud cheer from the other side of the curtain, followed by a shrill blast of party trumpets

and the pop of champagne.

'Oh,' I thought to myself, 'It must be a member of staff's birthday.' Wrong! The curtain was whipped back by a man I'd

___

never seen before. I tried to cover my pants with my hands but my palms were too small. Behind this grinning stranger were hundreds of people with glasses of champagne and paper streamers round their necks.

'Smile,' said a sweaty man with a camera. The flash went off in my face and everyone cheered. I was the millionth customer in the store and my great and glorious prize was to have my face and my pants on the front of every in-flight magazine on every plane that left Heathrow for the next ten years! Not only that, but this particular men's store had branches in every High Street in the country. So my picture was going nation-wide as well.

'Well, thanks,' I said to my mum.*

'Never mind,' she said. 'We got the suit free and at least this time you didn't have your finger sticking out your pants.'

'Didn't need to,' said William.

'What do you mean?' I said, as a hot flush rushed up my body. If it wasn't my finger . . .

Arrived at the cottage in Dunboyne outside Dublin, where Great Uncle Crawford was laid out in his coffin. Worst

Please, please, please don't let this have happened!

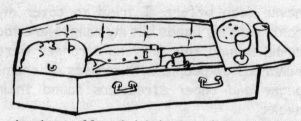

luck, the coffin *didn't* have a lid. Mum had to push me into the room where it was lying on top of the kitchen table. There were bottles and crisps and half-eaten sandwiches all round it and someone had put a sausage roll in Great Uncle Crawford's hand. He was as pale as a waxwork. He looked like eating that sausage roll might make him feel better.

Everyone was very friendly with drink, and they all wanted to know where Dad was. Mum had told us on the plane that we were just to say he was ill so as not to cause offence.

'Ill,' said Mum.

'How ill?' said Granny Constance. 'When I saw him on Saturday he wasn't too bad.'

'Very ill,' said Mum.

'He's going to die!' wailed my granny.*

'No, he's not,' said Mum.

'So what exactly has he got then?' asked Dad's sour-faced sister, Andrea. 'What has

290

he got that prevents him from hopping on an aeroplane like the rest of us and making an effort to see his own flesh and blood?'

Mum hesitated so I jumped in.

'Rabies,' I said.

Granny Constance gasped. Mum looked astonished. William and Mel groaned like I'd just let the side down again.

'They don't let you out of the country with rabies,' I said. It wasn't fair. I was only trying to help. Now everyone was staring at me.

'Dear God,' said Granny. 'The poor boy. How did he catch that?'

'Off the postman,' I said.

'The postman!'

'Who'd been bitten by a dog,' I added. Everything I said made it worse.

'Do the Post Office know?' asked Andrea's partner, Graham.

'Oh yes,' I said. 'They've put the dog down.'

'Have they?' he said. 'And the postman?'

'*And* the postman,' I said. 'Both of them at the same time. Double shot.' William and Mel put their heads in their hands. 'But

---

Dad was lucky apparently. He hasn't got the foam-at-the-mouth-and-turn-into-a-mad-fox type of rabies, he's just got the type of rabies where you can't fly to Ireland and see your family and you must stay in bed . . . watching telly.'

The thing about lying is some people are really good at it whereas I'm not. Nobody spoke to me for the rest of the day. I think they thought I was a little soft in the head.

Sat in the corner of the room watching everyone get drunk and dance to a fiddle and William's paper and comb. They were stuffing their faces with snacks and pies that Granny kept laying out alongside the coffin. Had plenty of time to think and was thinking, if there was a power failure and everyone was groping for food in the dark, what if I ate a finger by mistake thinking it was a carrot baton?*

Also I swear that Great Uncle Crawford was watching me. His eyes never left me all night. It was like they wanted something from me.

That night, William, Mel and I slept in one big bed. Mum was in another room. After my big brother and sister had told me a hundred times how stupid I was to open my mouth on the rabies thing, they took all the duvet and left me to freeze on the edge of the bed. The cold made me want the loo, so I got out of bed and put my foot in a metal bucket. The noise of me clumping around the room trying to shake off the bucket woke William and Mel.

'What are you doing?' they moaned.

'I'm trying to go to the loo, but it's dark and I don't know the way.'

'See that thing on your foot,' said Mel.

'This bucket?' I said.

'That is the loo,' she said. 'It's a potty.' No way was I going to the loo in *that*, not with my foot in it and not with Mel and William listening either!

Hopped back into bed and hung on.

As I lay there next to my big brother and sister, unable to sleep, listening to the night, I realized something. This cottage in

They'd probably record it and play it back to Pamela Whitby or something!

Ireland made scarier noises than our house in England; the wind outside that never stopped whining, the staircase that creaked like old bones, the roof that rustled with rats! But I wasn't scared. What was missing, as I lay there next to my big brother and sister, were the other noises, the thumping, the rattling, the eerie voices through the wall. As I lay there next to my big brother and sister a dim little light flickered to life in the back of my head.

4.30 a.m. – If they don't have a loo here with a flush and everything, maybe the burial's going to be a bit backward too. Maybe there'll just be four big men, two on the legs and two on the arms, swinging Great Dead Uncle Crawford's stiff little body as far away from the house as they can chuck it!

It is the morning of the funeral. I'm sitting up in bed. I'm worried I don't feel sad. If it's compulsory to cry at a funeral I'm in big trouble.

William and Mel had got all of the duvet again so slid out of bed to put on my clothes before I froze to death. Only I couldn't find them. I looked on the chair where I'd left them, under the chair, behind the chair, on the ceiling above the chair, but they weren't there. My new suit, my shirt, socks and black school shoes had disappeared! Only two people could have done this.

'Where is it?' I said.

'What?' said Mel.

'My suit. Ha-ha, hee-hee! My sides are split-ting! I'm only standing here with frostbite, aren't I?'

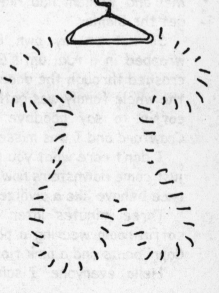

*I wish I'd brought an onion.*

295

'We don't know,' said William. 'Why would I want your suit anyway? I've got one of my own.'

When Mum found out she was furious. She said I'd deliberately lost my suit, because I hated it. And I wasn't wearing my jeans and showing her up. It was the suit or nothing.

William sniggered as he straightened his tie. 'So what are you going to wear? Bath mat? Curtain? Yellow trousers?'

Nothing. If I couldn't find my clothes I wasn't going. And when Mum found out that Mel and William had hidden them *they'd* get the blame.

So sat on my own in the bedroom, wrapped in a rug, until Granny Constance crashed through the door and told me that the whole family was gathered around the coffin to say goodbye to Great Uncle Crawford and I was missed.

'I don't care what you put on,' she spat,' just come downstairs now, Alistair, and for once behave like a civilized human being!'

Three minutes later walked into the coffin room wearing a pair of Mum's red Capri pants and a pink flowery blouse.

'Hello, everyone,' I said. 'I'm Alistair in

case you think I'm Mum. I'm sorry I'm late, but I've lost my sui . . .'

And then I saw it. It was wrapped around the dead body. Great Uncle Crawford was wearing it!

'I thought I heard footsteps coming up the stairs last night,' William whispered in my ear.

'Talia was right,' said Mel. 'You're a supernatural magnet. What with everything spooky at home and now this! If I were you, Alistair, I'd be very afraid.'

I was. I was very, very, VERY afraid! Because of me, the dead were walking!

While I stood terrified in the doorway, four men pushed past me and started to nail down the coffin lid. Mum rushed forward and hurled herself across the corpse like a grieving widow. Only she wasn't grieving. She was stripping the little old man of his clothes and handing them to me.

'Now you can nail it down,' she said to the undertakers, who stared at Mum like she was the meanest woman in the world for sending a man to his grave in his pants!

Then she told me to put my clothes on quickly or the funeral cars would have to go without me.

'I'm not wearing these,' I said, dropping the clothes on the floor. 'There's been a dead man in them! They're fish-cold! Feel them.'

But Granny Constance was in no mood for arguments. 'If you don't put them on,' she said, 'I'll bury you with Crawford!'

After wearing the clothes for ten minutes they didn't seem quite so cold. I opened the window of the limousine to let the smell of death escape and by the time we reached the church, the suit was almost comfortable. I say *almost* because I found a foreign fingernail in one of the pockets that made my flesh creep.

After the service the whole family stood around a hole in the graveyard while Great Uncle Crawford's coffin was lowered into the ground. This was when most people cried. Even William and Mel had their heads in their hands, so I copied what they were doing and jiggled my shoulders up and down to make it look like I was weeping.*

It was while I had my head lowered that I saw the dog under the tree. He was digging a hole in an old grave when suddenly he fell in and disappeared. Seconds later he re-emerged with several bones in his mouth. Then he ran over towards us, dropped them into Great Uncle Crawford's grave and went back for more. There was an embarrasses shuffling by the graveside as the family wondered what to do.

The priest was very good and tried to put everyone at their ease by cracking a funny joke. 'Well, Crawford will not be short of a nice drop of soup in the after-life!' he said to complete silence. Then realizing he'd made a bit of a blunder, he kicked the dog away and ordered the gravediggers to chuck in the soil to cover the bones from view.

But I had had a revelation. Bones and soup and dogs and graveyards! The Revengers had been looking for a grave-yard under the garden, but it was just Mum's soup bones that Mr E had dragged out the shed and scattered on the lawn. And if those terrifying bones weren't terrifying bones at all, then who was to say that the hauntings I heard every night weren't perfectly explainable too? Because there weren't any haunting noises last night. Not last night when Mel and William were sleeping in the same room as me and couldn't get out to *make* the noises!

300

Looked at Mel and William and realized they weren't crying at all. They were giggling.

It all makes sense now! How could I have been such a clump? Mum's new copper hood was scratched by a nail – one of Mel's nails that she'd stuck on for Andy! The Grim Reaper's scythe and his paper and comb voice – it was William on crutches! The clanking chain – that came from the loo. The scratching, the footsteps, the wailing, the laughter, the tapping on the wall – they were all Mel and William, paying me back for the voodoo dolls!

I am full of rage. To think how my mind has been twisted by terror that wasn't terror at all. This treachery by my big brother and sister demands a payback of humungous proportions! I shall not write anything else for a while. I must reserve my brainpower for the thinking up of evil.

Oh come, Revengers, come to me and we shall stuff them up big time!

# FRIDAY NIGHT

We're at the airport flying home. William and Mel do not suspect that I know a thing. I am hiding in the airport loos so that Mum cannot take me on another shopping spree. I think they're calling my flight.

## FRIDAY NIGHT @ HOME

When we got home, Mum found Dad in bed with a crate of beer.

'I wasn't expecting you home so early,' he said to Mum, trying to hide the bottles under his pillow.

Mum slept in the sitting room. There was a note on my bed from Dad.

*Mad Mrs Muttley phoned. Lock your windows and doors, son. She sounded slightly detached from reality.*
*Dad*

# SATURDAY

Woke up in my own bed. It's a weird day outside. It's swirling with fog and the street lamps are glowing yellowy-orange like firemen's torches in a blaze.

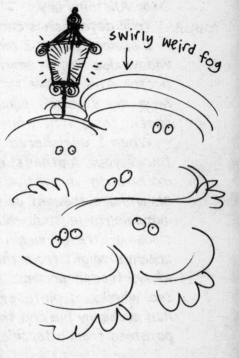

swirly weird fog

Mum and Dad are still not talking. Dad is pretending he's really ill again to make Mum feel sorry for him and forgive him his trespasses. But she's not happy that he pretended to be more ill than he really was just to get out of going to Ireland, so he could drink beer and watch sport uninterrupted.

Phoned Aaron and Ralph last night and they are coming round later this morning after I have done my detention for Pigeon.

Got to school to find this note pinned to the detention room door:

*Double yesssssss! She must have read my handwriting and cooked up some of my ingredients!

**So why's she in hospital if she's misread my disgusting ingredients as edible ones?

Dear Alistair Fury,

Yesssssss!    Your detention is cancelled.

I apologize, but I am unable to come in today due to a terrible sickness. The doctor says I have to go into hospital to have my stomach pumped, so I may be absent for a little while longer.*

When I deciphered your handwriting I found your mother's use of ingredients exceedingly innovative and bold. I would never have thought of using the following ingredients in soup, but they were delicious: a litre of virgin endive oil; clotted cream straight from the dairyman; cheesy whey; frozen prawns; six tablespoons of sea whelks; a plate of unwasted stocks; half a cherry pie and the burnt and crusty potatoes from a tortilla.**

Yours faithfully,
Miss Bird
    P.S. I miss my pet cat dreadfully, but she certainly livened up a leek and potato broth.

Ugh! Now I feel sick.
    The feeling got worse when I arrived home to find Mrs Muttley sitting at the

304

kitchen table. Slammed hands into pockets to hide fingers. She was crying and eating a whole packet of chocolate digestive biscuits. Mum was holding her hand.

'Do you like me teaching you the piano, Alistair?' blubbed Mrs Muttley. Her red wet cheeks wobbled with emotion. 'Only I'm not stupid. If you lose your fingers in a lawn mower accident you don't just *forget* to tell your piano teacher. I think you don't like me.'

'Look,' I cried, whipping out my fingers and wiggling them. 'It's a miracle. A surgeon just made me a new lot out of carrots and glue!'

excellent

But Mrs Muttley was no fool. She knew that carrots wouldn't work as fingers. One sniff of a cheese and chive dip and they'd be totally out of control. 'I've tried to make you love the piano,' she sobbed. 'I even came round a few nights ago and played Beethoven on the car stereo outside your bedroom window. I thought it might inspire you.' So that was the ghostly *Phantom* music that nearly scared me to death! This woman was a psycho! 'I don't want to lose you, Alistair. So I'm going to ask this question once and never again. Do you want to carry on playing the piano? If you say no I'll walk away and you'll never see me again, but if you say yes . . .' She looked at me with puppy dog eyes. '. . . if you say yes, you'll be rich and famous and own a yacht!'

I'll be honest here. Even though I knew she'd been practising that speech all the way over in the car, and only wanted me back for the sake of the £10 note I paid her every week, I still couldn't help being flattered. 'Wow, stardom!' I said. 'Yeah, sure! I'll carry on!' My one big chance to escape from tinkling her ivories and I blew it!

Later the Revengers came round for a Council of War. First we did the swearing in.

'I'm b***dy well going to kill them!'

'So am b***dy I.'

'And b***dy me!'

Then we sat around on the Carpet of War and discussed strategies. Ralph was all for tying bricks to Mel and William's shoes and chucking them in the river.

Aaron couldn't see the point. 'What harm have their shoes ever done us?' he said. 'I mean what's the point in drowning their shoes?'

'I was rather assuming that they'd be in them,' said Ralph.

'No,' I said. 'Not murder. They've been spooking me, so we've got to spook them back.'

'Well,' said Aaron, 'don't laugh, but I think this might work. We hire a pantomime horse costume and two of us get in it. Then the third one of us sits on top wearing a polo necked jumper which he pulls up over his head so it looks like he's headless. Then we ride around the garden wailing "whoo" and "waah".'

'I thought horses went neigh,' said Ralph.

'I was being the ghost,' said Aaron.

'I know,' said Ralph. We were getting nowhere fast.

Thinking up a haunting revenge was not as easy as it sounds. We bashed our brains together to think of a way for one of us to walk through a wall. That would be scary. But the only way we could think of walking through a wall was by using a door, and that

it's no good, it's locked

was pretty ordinary and not scary at all. Unless the door led to a room full of vampires or funnel web spiders, but we didn't have any of those.

After an hour of not having any good ideas, the doorbell rang. I went out onto the landing and leant over the banister to see who it was. The fog drifted in through the open door and floated around the hall as a man in a black overcoat stepped inside. He took off his hat and handed it to Mel.

In his other hand he had a doctor's bag.

'Alice,' called William. 'There's an exorcist here to see you.'

'What's an exorcist?' asked Aaron.

'He makes you puke up bad demons,' I said. 'Wait a minute! I've got it!'

'Got what?' said the others. They looked scared, like they half expected a little red man with a forked beard, sharp horns and a long pointy tail to shoot out of my mouth!

'Got the revenge!' I said. 'I bet you a million pounds that this exorcist is another of William and Mel's scams. So why don't we scam them back!'

Aaron and Ralph nodded. 'How?' said Ralph.

'We're going to need a dead body,' I said.

very concerned

The exorcist was waiting in the hall with a serious face. He took my hand, shuddered like I was repulsive to him and uttered these words. 'Time is short. We must hurry.'

It seemed I was indeed possessed and needed help immediately. Mel sent Aaron and Ralph home telling them that what was about to happen was far too gruesome for human eyes.

'That's what we were hoping,' said Ralph. 'Can't we stay?'

'We won't say a word,' said Aaron.

'No,' said Mel, pushing them out the door and slamming it shut.

We cleared the kitchen table and I lay down.

'I need herbs and a live chicken,' said the exorcist. 'Switch off the lights, close all the windows and nobody touch the kettle. We don't have tea till we're done! Tell me honestly, Alistair, does your head rotate the full three hundred and sixty degrees? Is your vomit green? Does your hair fall

310

into tangles? Do your eyes glow red in a demonic sort of way?'

'No,' I said. 'Never!' I put on a faraway kind of voice as if I was entering a trance, just to get everyone in the mood.

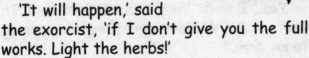

'It will happen,' said the exorcist, 'if I don't give you the full works. Light the herbs!'

'I couldn't find any,' said William. 'I got a bouquet garni instead.'

'I can't light that,' said the exorcist, 'I'll start a fire.' He seemed disappointed. 'Cut the chicken's neck and pour the blood over Alistair's head!'

That's herbs in a bag

William laughed nervously.

'It's a frozen chicken,' he said. 'No blood.' So they rubbed the frozen giblets in my hair, which was quite uncomfortable actually and made

---

my scalp ache from the cold.

Then the exorcist took some candles from his bag and stuck one to each corner of the table. He took out some chalk and drew a star on the floor.

'Are you scared yet?' asked William. So this was why Mel and William were doing this. To see how far they could go before I cried and begged them to stop.

'Yes,' I said. 'Very scared. Petrified. In fact . . . Oh, William, something's happening to my arm.'

'What is it?' said Mel. 'You're turning blue. Alistair, what are you doing?'

'I think I'm . . .' I stuttered a bit like the words wouldn't come out. I blew bubbles of spit out my mouth. And then I died.

'Alistair?' That was William. 'Alistair!'

'ALISTAIR!' That was Mel. 'What's happened? He's stopped breathing!'*

# 'YOU'VE KILLED HIM.'

'I haven't killed him,' said the exorcist. 'I haven't touched him.'

'Well, make him better.'

'How can I make him better? I'm a media student.' And he threw off his exorcist wig and stormed out of the front door. I recognized him as one of Mel's A-level mates.

# 'WHAT ARE WE GOING TO DO?'

she shouted.

make Amends

'Make amends,' said a ghostly voice through the kitchen window. Mel and William froze in terror as the voice echoed up from the bowels of the earth. 'Repent! Give up your wordly goods!'

Then they both started crying! It was brilliant.

'Put the money from both of your bank accounts – that's *all* your allowance mind you, not half – into Alistair's Post Office account immediately! If you do not, I, Trog the Mighty Ghost of Revenge, will personally do you in. William, be nice to your younger brother from now on. Mel, never put your clothes in his wardrobe again . . .'

Unfortunately Mel and William had twigged us. They pulled open the back door and found Aaron and Ralph under the window, shouting into a tin bucket.

'Ho-ho-ho!' said my big brother and sister. 'Very funny! Most amusing! You can open your eyes now, Alice.' I opened my eyes. 'Did you really expect us to fall for that old joke?'

'Yes,' I said. 'And you did.'

That was when we all heard a loud knock on the inside of the larder door.

'Oh what a wizard wheeze!' mocked

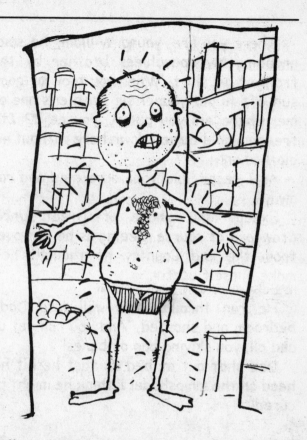

William. 'You've got Mum in on this as well have you? Planted her in the larder?'

'No,' I said, because I hadn't. Then the larder door swung open and standing by the onions was Great Uncle Crawford wearing only the underpants we buried him in. His skin was bright blue.

'There you are, young William,' he said, grabbing my speechless brother by the front of his shirt. 'When you took my good suit off to put your little brother's one on me, where did you put it, you eejit? It's freezing cold buried down here without my clothes on!'

As I recall, everyone screamed and ran away!

Except the ghost of Great Uncle Crawford of course. Seeing as he was over from the Old Country he thought he'd make himself useful.

He'd always had a soft spot for Mum.

He ran through the wall into Dad's bedroom and shouted, 'And you can get up and all, you skiving bag of bones!'

Dad shot out of bed so fast he hit his head on the lampshade! I think he might be cured!

Spent day on loo making nervous bum soup.

Dad has gone back to work. Mum is singing. Great Uncle Crawford has got his suit and is back in the ground. Everything is back to normal.

Complimentary copy of in-flight magazine arrived from the men's store at Heathrow Airport. Joy! The photo of me on the front cover is a head and shoulders shot. You can't see below my neck, so I'll never know if my willy was sticking out of the front of my trousers or not! I can once again rejoin the human race with my dignity intact.

# CHEWSDAY

Mel finally went out on her date with Andy. Sadly her rich, hotshot lover-boy turned out to be a very ordinary cheapskate.
I can't think why!

Apparently, Andy received an anonymous phone call telling him that Mel was a simple girl who hated glitz and glamour. If he was thinking of taking her to the Ritz he should cancel immediately, because she hated all that lovely food and chandeliers and famous people at the next tables. If he really wanted to impress her he should take her to a Pizza Hut, let her pay for her own meal afterwards, dump her at the bus stop to make her own way home! Don't think we'll be seeing Andy again!

Is that so, Alice? I thought you might be plotting something like this, you little toad? Well, two can play at that game.
Your loving sister
Mel

0/10

This diary is the shoddiest piece of work I have seen for ages. Appalling spelling and flouts every grammatical rule in the book. You have obviously NOT been paying attention in my English lessons. SATURDAY MORNING DETENTIONS TILL THE END OF YOUR SCHOOL LIFE! You have a lovely sister and should be grateful that she brought me your diary. I know I am.

Pigeon

# DON'T MISS

**Alistair's next brilliant revenge in**

# THE WAR DIARIES OF ALISTAIR FURY

## The Kiss of Death

**Read an extract now – see over!**

Here is a list of most-hated people in history:

**Genghis Khan**
**Jack the Ripper**
**Adolf Hitler**
**Alistair Fury**

What do they all have in common? They all had sofas in their bedrooms.

'Is it true?' said Aaron.

'It must be,' I said. 'Ever since my new sofa was delivered, William and Mel have hated me because I won't let them use it for snogging sessions.' Actually this was the only reason I got the sofa in the first place – to annoy my big brother and sister. And also because Ralph had said it was time us Revengers got into kissing.

Not each other, of course. I checked with Ralph and he didn't mean in that way at all.

Ralph has changed. His body is sprouting hairs like the way blotting-paper sprouts watercress in Reception Class. And he uses a deodorant now at week-ends. We were meeting in our secret bus shelter by the McDrive-In, because Ralph had brought along a Shower Catalogue and didn't want anyone seeing us looking at it.

'What's so naughty about showers?' I asked. He turned the page to a picture of a naked woman behind a shower curtain. You could see her ankles and shower cap. I tried to look at the bath mat and pretend I wasn't interested, but my eyes kept drifting upwards. My mouth went dry and my heart beat so loudly that everyone in the street could hear it. I had to think of the most boring thing in the universe to stop the noise. I thought of French vocab:

*Le can-can* is a bird called a 'toucan'.

*Mon père a un moustache* 'my pear has a moustache'.

*Le chat* is 'the chat' as in the common phrase, *Un telephone chat-line*.

We Revengers have a secret code to stop us talking if a stranger stands next to us and waits for a bus. The secret code is 'Shhhhh'. Sometimes buses pull in to pick us up and drivers get angry when we don't get on. A bus stopped today and the driver was a psychopath. He had scary sideburns growing out of his mouth. So we got on and held the rest of our meeting at the back of the bus in little fairy whispers.

I wanted to know how Ralph thought we were going to get a kiss when none of us knew any girls who weren't our sisters or cousins.

'Girls prefer to kiss people they don't know,' he said, 'because they don't know enough about you to hate you yet.'

'Yeah, but if you don't know them,' I said, 'how can you ask for a kiss?'

'You don't ask,' said Ralph, 'you trick them. You pretend you're dying and need the kiss of life. Or switch the lights off at a party and steal a kiss in the dark. Or tell her you're a spy like James Bond and have to pass her a secret message mouth to mouth!'

The party sounded most practical. Trouble was, none of us had ever thrown one before. We weren't exactly sure what to do. We knew we had to move all the furniture against the walls and put newspaper on the floor, but we didn't know why.

'Do people bring their pets to parties?' asked Aaron.

'Maybe the newspaper's there to give you something to read while you're kissing,' said Ralph.

'When it gets boring, you mean? Because I have heard,' I said, 'that some kisses can go on for so long that worried parents report their children as missing.'

Aaron and Ralph wanted to have the kissing party as soon as possible. 'Next Sunday, your place,' they said.

'Can't,' I said. 'Next Sunday is Mum's new cookbook launch.'

'Saturday then,' said Ralph.

'Mrs Muttley's piano concert,' I said.

They accused me of making excuses because I was scared of kissing, but I really am that busy next weekend.

'Then when can we come?' said a disappointed Ralph.

'In about five years,' I said. 'When Mum isn't precious about her new kitchen any more.'

Mum's just had a new kitchen fitted for her TV show. The lights are so bright that it makes us all sweat like heavyweight boxers, which is nice in the food. 'Mmmm! What's on the Sweat Trolley tonight, Mum?'

Walked five miles home after bus conductor threw us off the bus for not having any money to pay our fares. The three of us are now outlaws, which is good because girls love bad boys.

At home my big brother and sister were waiting for me. Both wanted to borrow my sofa tonight as they'd got hot-totty lined up. But when I said no, they said, 'Right, you tightwad, you're dead!' Which was a nice thing to say on the holiest day of the week.

Mel's current boyfriend is called Roger. She never stops telling us how beautiful he

is, but he's got spots like a Chelsea Bun and nasty cheap trainers, which is why I secretly call him Roger the Todger. He gave Mel a bracelet made from hairs that grow on top of an elephant's head and she thinks it's a sign of endless love. It's a sign of endless bald elephants, stupid!

As if I didn't suffer enough in the first diary!

WIGS R US XXL

WIG GLUE

William thinks he's a babe magnet because he says he's got more girlfriends than all of Westlife put together.

He's not a magnet. He's fly-paper and it's all the dirty flies what nobody else wants who stick to him! The present girlfriend is a bad-tempered blue-bottle called Rosie.

# GRANNY GO HOME

# HORROR!

Granny Constance blew in for Sunday supper like a cold arctic wind. She doesn't like me. In fact there's not much she does like, except nattering on about her aches and pains, and her Scrabble Club, which she thinks is the centre of the universe. Like we should all care deeply that Elsie made 'carbuncle' last week on a triple-word score using a 'car' that was already down there!

'Not a real car, you understand, just the word,' she kept saying.

'Yes, Granny! For the fifty millionth time, I'd worked that out for myself!'

We don't eat Sunday lunch in the Fury household. That would be too normal. Because my mum is a TV chef we have to eat at supper, and never beef or lamb, always disgusting food like sturgeon and chicken livers and raw goat in gravy. Today it is pheasant. Yuck!

## ONE OF LIFE'S LITTLE PROBLEMS

Tomorrow I have a French test with Miss Bird. She calls it her *Grand Examination de French*. Here is an actual conversation I once had with a French teacher:

'J'ai numque been any bonbon a French.'

'Paraquat?'

'Because I can't see the point of it. Everyone speaks English where I live.'

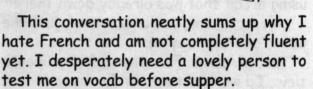

This conversation neatly sums up why I hate French and am not completely fluent yet. I desperately need a lovely person to test me on vocab before supper.

Could I find a lovely person to help me? William and Mel would rather I died than got a proper education, Mum's too busy phoning round for a duck-billed platypus – not to eat, just to put on display at her book launch next week – and Dad's too busy

who said I couldn't draw a platy...thing?

tiling. He's gone DIY mad. It's pathetic. It's taken him a whole week to stick up one tiny square of tiles behind the sink in the new kitchen! I think DIY must stand for 'Dad Is Yelling!' because every time he cuts

← even thugs are shocked

himself he swears really loudly. It's brilliant! When he's shouting **s*i*g*t** and **p*ck**q**m*s** and **f***yw**g*e** I can swear as much as I like and nobody can hear me!

Mum's launch party's got an Australian Beach Barbecue theme because her new book is called *Playing with Fire – Cooking in the Great Outdoors*. She says that if this book doesn't sell well, we'll have to live in a rented caravan and eat fish skins and pig trotters for the rest of our lives. That's

why it's so important that this party's a success. Everyone who I've never heard of is coming and a man called Cornelius is helping to organize it. He's an inferior designer, which probably means he's cheap.

Anyway, it turned out that the only person who was free to help me with my French homework was Granny. So I said in my loudest most sarcastic voice, 'Oh thank you, Granny. At least one of my family loves me. I wish you lived here all the time instead of my real family.'

But Granny was just as selfish as the rest.

'Ask me words in French first,' I said.

'Cowpat,' she said. 'That's another good one. Thirty-six on a triple-word score.' Her mind is Scrabbled.

While Dad was carving the pheasant there was an unsavoury incident. Mr E, our pug dog, jumped on a chair and shoved his ugly mug into the puddle of blood that was lapping round the bird like a moat. Then he started drinking. I think Mr E is a Vampire Dog. If I was to hit him with a cricket bat he'd explode with blood like a mosquito. Dad only noticed when the pheasant started moving, floating slowly across the meat plate towards the dog's sucking mouth. Mr E caught a flick with an oven glove right up his bum, which made him squeal and run off into the garden.

Granny said, 'That dog's disgusting. And that clumsy cat's no better.'

Our cat, Napoleon, had his tail chopped off in a cat flap, which means he's always falling over. When the builders were here rebuilding the back of the house they had to wear hard hats all the time because Napoleon kept plunging off the scaffolding.

mmm...be raining cats and dogs before long

Granny gave me a book called *How to Hypnotize Your Pet into Better Behaviour* and said it was my job to cure our pets.

an ex
pheasant

'Why me?' I said.

'Because your brain is the most beastly in the family,' said Granny.

Don't think calling me an animal is particularly funny. Do I go to the loo in the park where everyone can see me? No. Not for a long time now.

The pheasant was full of bullets. Granny choked on one and coughed her potatoes onto my plate. I was told not to make a fuss.

see, I'm telling the TOOTH!!

'But there's two teeth in my peas,' I said.

'Don't be so stupid,' said Granny, taking her dentures back off my plate, 'there's no t in peas.'

# THE WAR DIARIES OF ALISTAIR FURY

## Exam Fever

### Jamie Rix

AAAAAAAAAGH

Sharpen pencils, dust off lucky gonk and feel sick!  It's exam time!!!

TEST FOR ALISTAIR

1. How can I stop mum and dad discovering that I am the thickest one in the family? a) Cheat at all my exams. b) Change my family. c) Make big brother and sister fail their exams too.

2. Should Mum shave the beard off a goat before she cooks it for her latest TV chef project? a) Yes, because whiskers are difficult pick out of your teeth. b) Don't care, because I'm never eating goat. c) No, because the beard soaks up the gravy.

Answers to be found in this hilarious instalment of
Alistair's diaries of revenge.

CORGI YEARLING BOOKS
ISBN 0 440 86592 1

# THE WAR DIARIES OF ALISTAIR FURY

## Summer Helliday

### Jamie Rix

It's the holidays!

School's broken up and I've got the chance to be a celebrity – at last! There's a film audition in my neighbourhood and I'm determined to get the main part. Mum wants to drag me off on a family caravan holiday with Granny but that clapped-out old toilet-on-wheels won't come between me and super-stardom. Nor will the caravan.

My big brother and sister want to ruin my chance of fame but I've got friends in high places, and I'm not just talking about Mr E when he's on top of a skip.

So watch out, Mel and William! RIP – Revenge is Planned in another outrageous episode in Alistair's catalogue of revenge.

CORGI YEARLING BOOKS
ISBN 0 440 86591 3